Poppie

Angel DeVille

Published by Angel DeVille, 2024.

POPPIE

First edition. September 10, 2024.

ISBN: 979-8227905635

Written by Angel DeVille.

Table of Contents

Chapter 1 - Reality

Poppie

It didn't have to be this way. Unfortunately, I didn't have a choice in the matter. However, everything happens for a reason. Why this shit happened to me, I really don't know.

I didn't ask to be born, but I was. I didn't really have a fucking choice. And here I am trying to figure out my life, without any directions.

I aged out of the system, so I've been on my own since I was 18 yrs old. Here I am 5 yrs later, still struggling just as hard as I did when I was in the facility.

I got my friend, Shayla, who helps me out from time to time. She hooked me up with the temp job she works with, so I make money, just not a lot. Right now, I have a studio apartment but by the way shit keeps happening, I may be losing it too. Rent seems to be going up across the city and my landlord is an asshole.

I don't know if he actually owns the building or if he just works for the person who does but this motherfucker gets on my last nerves. Every time he sees me, he always smiles and calls me "Snowflake". Like I'm the only white girl living in the fucking building. I think just because I'm young, he thinks I don't know when I'm being preyed upon. I know he wants to fuck me, I can tell how he looks at me. I don't want to go down that road with him because I know that road won't end well.

It's 5:00 am and I gotta get my ass ready for work. I didn't think I would be working in an office, but Shayla helped me with my resume and the temp agency. They have been keeping me busy with a job, but since I don't have many skills, I don't get the opportunity to get paid that much. White privilege my ass, ain't none of that shit going on here. I think that shit hit differently anyway, because that shit only works for the white people with money, because my bitch ass has been white since I was born and I've been struggling since I could remember.

I don't even know my mom or dad. I think they weren't ready for a kid so they left me behind to live their lives. Who knows? I don't give a fuck really because they didn't give a fuck about me. They just wanted to fuck and have fun without all the consequences of said fuck.

As I look in the mirror while I'm brushing my teeth, I see another freckle has popped up on my face. This one is above my left eyebrow. I don't have a lot of freckles but a few have dotted my face over the years. They match my red curly hair that flows down my back. I don't know which of my parents gave me red hair but it makes me fucking noticeable.

I stared into the mirror, looking myself directly into my hazel eyes, wishing my life was just a little bit different. I was so alone, I had no one. Then my phone rang.

It was Shayla. I had at least one person.

"Hey Shayla." I answered after spitting out my toothpaste.

"Hey Bitch, how you?"

"Tired as fuck. I don't wanna go to work today."

"I know, but that party was lit last night, right?"

"Yeah it was, but why you have it in the middle of the fucking week?"

"Shit, I didn't even know all them damn people were coming through," she said as I heard start the car. She was on her way to come and pick me up. "Mike ain't tell me shit. He knew but didn't let me know nothing."

"It's all good, it was fun, I'm just tired as fuck right now."

"Well Bitch, wake the fuck up, take you a hit and get ready cuz a Bitch is on the way."

"You gonna have time to smoke?"

"Shit, watchu think? I gotta start the day right, so yes I will."

"A'ight. I'll have it rolled up by the time you get here." I disconnected the phone and left the bathroom.

Shayla was a friend who I had known all my life in the facility. She got out about 2 years before me, as her aunt let her come and live with her but we would hang everyday. Her boyfriend, Mike, who was a bit older than us, had a place for us to hang out. He would come around the facility to pick Shayla up from time to time. When she had to leave, she told me she would come back for me and she kept her promise.

Shayla was the only person who would look after me. We were always together like sisters. We were together so much, the staff thought we were really sisters. We didn't tell them differently, because it didn't matter. To me, she was my big sister because she took care of me like a big sister would, even though we were the same age.

I twisted my hair up into a messy bun and grabbed my Rick & Morty stash can so I could roll a couple of blunts for us to smoke. As soon as I opened the top the beautiful smell of ganja, whiffed across my nose. It was some good shit.

Just as I finished rolling the second blunt, the doorbell buzzed - Shayla had made it over. I buzzed her in as I lit one of the blunts. While I inhaled deeply, the 'cherry' glowed an amber red.

Shayla walked through the door dressed to impress for her job. She stood about 5'5", shapely with hips, thick thighs and fat ass. Her smooth butter pecan colored skin glowed as she had used the body butter with glitter. I could see her skin shine as she sat down on the only couch I could put in this place.

"Good morning. You looking good and smelling good."

"Thank you Boo," she said as she received the blunt I passed. "I was like let me look at least decent today cuz a Bitch is tired too." Shayla inhaled on the blunt and closed her eyes.

"I feel you. I got this outfit for today," I said, holding up a pair of black slacks and a royal blue blouse with white polka dots and short, puffy sleeves.

"Oh that's cute. That will bring out your freckles. You always look good in blue." Shayla said as she passed the blunt to me.

"Thanks. So what y'all doing this weekend? Y'all having another party?"

"Yeah girl. Mike got some of his guys coming in from out of town so he wants to have a nice party so he can sell and we can make some money."

"Well I will be there. I need to get my shit tapped just right."

"Yeah, them fuckers last night wasn't into shit but smoking and bones. I think they were gay." Shayla said and I almost choked.

Mike and Shayla have these parties from time to time called *'Play Parties'*. A select group of people are invited over to their house where we have a nice get-together were we drink, Mike sells a selection of goodies and sometimes, there would be some guys who want to fuck.

That's where me and Shayla would come in. Mike and Shayla were swingers so Mike didn't give a fuck what or who Shayla did as long as she was loyal to him. When it came time to fuck, they had to pay up front before they get to tap.

It really didn't matter to me honestly, it was just sex. I have no connection with anyone in that department to even think past fucking. It's just temporary pleasure and I get paid. I've never felt anything for anyone and I didn't plan to, so there was no need for me to catch any kind of feelings with any of them motherfuckers. They only saw me as a piece of ass anyway.

"Why you think that?" I finally managed to get out.

"Cuz they weren't trying to hit shit, they weren't into pussy. They wanted to ride and spin on the pole." Shayla said in between the puffs of the blunt. "They wanted to bust a nut into a niggas mouth while riding."

"Yo ass stupid as fuck!" I laughed and Shayla joined.

"You know they was Bitch, you know I'm telling the truth."

"They were looking at Mike pretty hard. One kept following Mike throughout the house."

"Yeah Mike told me about him. He *was* gay. Mike had been knowing him for a while but he thought he would bring at least a few straight niggas to come and play. But this nigga only came with gay motherfuckers looking to get their dick sucked while getting fucked."

"Well gay people need love too."

"True, but damn. I really wanted to make some *dollas* last night."

"I feel you, so did I."

Chapter 2 - Meet Austin

Poppie

By the time the weekend came around, I was fucking ready to party. I had complained the entire week that I was dog-tired but when Friday came around? *A Bitch was not tired at all.* Shayla said that the party would start around 9 pm, which meant I would arrive around 10 pm.

I had dressed in my best outfit, a light blue jean mini skirt, multi-colored striped halter top and nice pair of kicks - a pair of Timbs. The fall had come in like a beast in Chicago which meant winter wasn't far behind. In Chicago, it seemed as though seasons were bipolar because it could be hot one day and cold the next. I didn't need to get sick because I couldn't afford to miss any work.

Shayla and Mike's place wasn't far from me as I could walk, but with it being cold I needed to catch an uber over to their place. I used almost the last of the money I had until payday next week, which meant I needed to make some cash tonight.

When I pulled up to the house, I could hear the music bumping outside. There were a few guys hanging outside smoking cigs in the cold. Mike and Shayla smoke weed but they don't like the cigarette smell so those that smoke cigs, had to brave the cold for those much needed squares. I jumped out of the car and walked towards the house and got the attention of the guys outside.

"Yo, look at this thick ass white girl coming ova here," Dude number one said. He looked like John Legend's little brother with his light brown skin and almond eyes.

I ignored him and kept walking towards the house. I felt all eyes on me as I got closer to the door.

"Wassup up Snow Bunny, you coming to play?"

I always got '*Snow Bunny or Snowflake*' as a nickname because I'm white. It didn't bother me, but I'm like y'all can't come up with something better?

"You coming to pay?" I gave so much attitude. Shayla swears I must have been Black in a past life.

"'Oooo shit, she got you dude." Dude number two said as I walked past him going up the stairs.

"You for sale?"

"Depends on who's buying and if you can afford me, because I know I'm worth it." I smacked my lips and looked at him.

"Day-um dude."

"It's like that Shorty?"

"You already know it is. Don't think I'm stupid because I'm white, I know how to deal with slick motherfuckas like you." I pointed in their direction.

"A'ight. Ok Amber with the red hair."

"Funny," I rolled my eyes. "It's Poppie with the freckles," I said as I opened the door, walked in and closed the door quickly behind me.

"Poppie! Wassup girl!" Shayla said as she was coming from the kitchen with a bottle of Hennessy.

"Hey, who are those fools outside?"

"Oh, that must be Mike's cousins, don't mind them, they ain't got shit." I nodded and hung my coat in the closet.

Mike and a few guys were in the dining room playing bones like always. He knows he loves playing dominoes. As I looked around, there was a bunch of people in the fucking house. There was a gang of people all over the place. I walked into the living room and there were a few people I recognized - Shayla's cousin Tanya and her girlfriend, Stephanie.

"Heeeeyyyy Poppie! My favorite white girl!" Tanya said as she got up to give me a hug.

"I ain't seen you in a minute, how you been?"

"Shit you know, making it do what it do," I said. "Hey Stephanie."

"Hey Poppie." Stephanie didn't talk much, she was always watching Tanya to make sure she wasn't stepping out on her. She was *really* insecure. They had been together for at least 5 years but I guess there is a trust issue, I don't know.

"Well I'm glad you here cuz we need to get a card game going. I'm ready to play some spades and get my drink on." Stephanie laughed.

"A'ight, let me get a drink and I'll be back," I said as I walked to the kitchen.

I waved to a few people on the way. There were a few people I recognized, basically from them being more so customers of Mike. Mike has been slinging as long as I've known Shayla. I only get weed from him through Shayla, which means I don't pay for shit. I don't deal with all of that other shit, I'm good with just weed. But I must admit Mike does have a good selection of shit if anyone wanted to get high - he could get you fucking lifted.

I walked into the kitchen, where the drinks were lined up on the counter like a bar. I went straight to the red solo cups, picked up a cup and grabbed the Crown Royal Apple.

"You gonna need this little mama," a deep voice said behind me. I turned around and there stood this sexy ass motherfucker looking like Boris Kodjoe, holding a gallon of apple juice. Smooth, peanut butter skin, nice ass face and a fucking amazing body.

"Yes, I will need that." I wasn't implying the apple juice.

"Let me help you," he said as took the CR out of my hands. "You want ice?"

"Yeah, a few cubes will be nice," I said looking at him. He winked and smiled at me as he poured the liquor in my cup.

"Tell me when," he said as he poured. I watched it get about a third of the way up the cup.

"That's good."

"Okay, here's the ice," he said as he dropped a few cubes in my cup. I immediately swished my drink around and took a sip. His eyebrows raised as he watched me. "You want it straight?"

"Is that how you give it?" I had a smart ass mouth and I knew it. It made him blush but he controlled it.

"Oh, I'll give it any way you want it." This was the type of motherfucker I wanted to hook up with, but was he willing to pay for it?

"Oh really? I don't give refunds."

"That's cool. I don't mind paying extra." I blinked hard. He came to play as he continued to stare. His green eyes were mesmerizing and I felt myself getting lost in them.

"Okay. I like what I hear," I said, holding up my cup waiting for the apple juice to be added as we got off subject. "You gonna give me some juice?"

"As much as you want," he said, grabbing the juice to pour into my cup. "So what's your name?"

"Poppie. What's yours?"

"Austin, nice to meet you Poppie."

"Nice to meet you too Austin." Austin put the juice on the counter and picked up a cup to make himself a drink.

"So how you know Mike and Shayla?"

"Shit, me and Shayla go way back, she's like my sister."

"Oh, I know you. You're Poppie, the one Mike has been telling me about. You grew up with Shayla right?"

"Yup, that's me. How you know Mike?"

"Mike is my nigga, we went to school together."

"Oh ok, that's cool."

"Cheers," he said, holding up his cup. We clinked cups and took a sip.

"You always come to their parties?"

"Yes and no. I usually come over to hang with Shayla and smoke. Sometimes I play, sometimes I don't. Sometimes I come over 'cause I ain't got shit to do."

"I feel you on that. I just got into town. I was thinking about moving back."

"Oh, so where you live now?"

"Miami."

"Fuck, Miami! That's nice. I ain't never been, but always wanted to go."

"Well maybe you can come and visit sometime," he offered. The invitation was nice, but a Bitch ain't got money for a fucking plane ticket. Unless this motherfucker is paying, I ain't going nowhere.

"That would be nice, but I don't make money like that at my temp piece of shit job to get a ticket."

"No worries, I got you." My eyes got big and I raised my eyebrows in bewilderment. *Did this mofo just tell me he was going to pay for my trip?*

"POPPIE! Bring yo ass so we can play Spades and beat these Bitches!" Shayla yelled from the living room.

"That's my queue. I'm Shayla's partner for Spades."

"Oh ok, well I'll see you later on," he said smiling while reaching for my hand. He held it up to his mouth and slowly kissed the back of my hand, keeping eye contact with me.

I blushed. "You promise?"

"Fo' sho baby girl."

This motherfucker had me in a daze. I smiled and slowly strolled out the kitchen to the living room where the table was set up with the game ready to go.

"So I see you met Austin," Shayla said as she placed the deck of cards in front of Tanya to cut.

"Yeah, that motherfucka is fine as fuck."

"I know right. Mike told me that he was coming and that he told him about you."

"Shut the fuck up. Mike told him about me?"

"Girl yeah, he was like if anyone should get with him, it should be you. Dude got money. He used to play basketball."

"For what team?" I said, as I watched Shayla pick up the stack after Tanya finished cutting the deck and dealt them out.

"He didn't make the NBA, but he made the G-league and has been playing overseas."

"Aw damn, okay. At least he is still playing," I said as I picked up my cards and rearranged my hand.

"I know right. But he had been asking about you since he arrived."

"Damn okay." I sang. He was looking for me.

"Y'all Bitches gonna play and stop all this damn talking?"

"Why the fuck you worried about it Tanya, y'all gonna lose anyway?" Shayla said, slamming down the ace of diamonds.

"Shut the fuck up," she said playing her card.

"You know y'all gonna get her mad and I gotta go home with her," Stephanie said as she played her card.

"'That Bitch can't play, that's why she get mad." Shayla said as I played with 2 of diamonds.

"I ain't gonna be mad, 'cause we're gonna fucking win," Tanya said as she slammed down a 2 of Spades.

Shayla and I just looked at each other 'cause this Bitch just fucked up our strategy. Stephanie started smiling while Tanya danced around as she took our *'book'*. This was going to be an interesting game and night, I see.

Chapter 3 - Mix

Vanessa

I was born a business woman. A woman with stature and grace, yet a wolf when it comes to running a business and making it grow. My father raised me without knowing he did. I watched him from afar. He didn't want me to run the family business. He wanted me to marry well to be able to merge with another company. He saw me as an asset to build a business. I saw him for who he was - a man using a woman for financial gain.

My mother wasn't phased by it at all. She enjoyed the lavish life and she didn't give a fuck what my father did. She had her guy on the side as did my father, who would meet up with his significant other, outside the home.

They catered to my brother as he would run the family business and I would inherit a few properties, however, I would not have a deciding opinion when it came to the business. So I decided to build my own, doing what I love to do best.

After my husband of 7 yrs died and left me alone with our adopted son, Samuel, I decided I would live my life away from the spotlight of what my father and brother owned. I was married and became a widow at the young age of 28. Therefore I decided to build my business with my escort service.

After being around the limelight of my father, who was always entertaining the wealthy, I understood what most of them wanted. Some wanted companionship and others wanted friends with benefits. I understood the game and I learned how to play it well.

I learned so well that I now own one of the most extravagant escort services in Chicago. It's called Elegant Escorts/Distinct Women. Elegant Escorts are women who have been educated on how to be the companion for the high profile individual who needs to attend an important event or if they are in town for business and they need a companion for the duration of their trip. Sex is not included as they are strictly escorts who offer professional companionship.

The women are educated in various languages depending on the client's needs. They are fully diverse in law, medicine and other topics as needed. They are able to hold a very intellectual conversation with Heads of State if need be. I pride myself on making sure the women are educated in various fields and languages and they are compensated well.

Now there are times in which certain individuals would like a bit more from their companions. Distinct Women are women who are companions and sexual partners, depending on the taste and lifestyle of the individual. They are still held to the same standards of the Elegant Escorts, the only thing different is that sex may be involved.

I've been doing this since my husband passed away 22 years ago. I've been making a name for myself the best way I know how.

Now, I am in need of a few more ladies as a few of them have gone on to do better things. Some ladies come to make their money and disappear and I'm fine with that. They can always come back if they need. Others stay around and make their money and invest their money so when they leave, they don't have to return.They have learned to make what they have work for them. These girls grow into women with businesses and hold themselves to a higher standard than most. They know how to play that Men's game and I've taught them to play it well.

As I said before, I need to replace a few girls in the hopes to grow new ladies. And maybe even find a woman that may interest my son Samuel. He is what keeps me going daily. Even though he's 25 ys of age, I still worry about him finding the right one.

Samuel is unique. We all have our little quirks about us. It is what makes us - us. Those who truly love us, understand and learn to adapt. I am trying to find someone who is capable of doing that with Samuel.

"Mr. Peabody, I need to find at least 2 additional girls and no more than 5. Is that understood?"

"Yes Ma'am."

"How are the others doing?"

"They are doing well Ma'am. Everyone is booked for the weekend."

"Good to hear. We shall finally have some time."

"Yes we shall."

When the weekends are booked, it finally leaves time for me to relax and not worry about the girls. Mr. Peabody is the equivalent of my right arm. He runs the company along with me as my assistant. If anything should ever happen, he knows exactly how to keep this place running until my return.

As I got myself together to head into the office, an old flame decided to give a call.

"Hello Vanessa. It's been too long."

"It has Governor Fitzgerald, how are you?"

"I'm doing well, thank you. Vanessa, I'm calling you because I have my grandson coming into Chicago and he would need your services. He will be there for a charity event for his fraternity."

"Understood Governor. I will be happy to help. Your grandson, you say? Is this Richard?"

"Yes, it is. He has grown to be such a young man now. He's 23 yrs old now."

"Oh I'm sure you had a hand in that." he giggled at the flattery. I deal with political figures who want to find just the right person to share an evening with, without all of the stories that go along with it.

They have a reputation to uphold. I simply help them with companionship. As long as the guys don't get out of hand, everything will go well.

"Yes, I can say so myself. I trust you will handle everything accordingly?"

"Of course, you can most definitely trust me with that. How many will be joining us?"

"It will be 7 young men, all the same age, who will be attending the charity event."

"Great. We shall send a car with their companion to pick them up. I'll have Mr. Peabody reach out to you to get the contracts signed and to go over all the details."

"Fabulous. I knew I could always count on you Vanessa," he said, sounding proud and assured.

"Always Governor. It was a pleasure hearing from you."

"Thank you Vanessa. It was good speaking with you."

The Governor disconnected and I looked at Mr. Peabody.

"You already know what to do, correct?"

"Yes, I'll go over 8 just to have a back up."

"Make it 9, just in case."

As I said before, I pride myself in my business. Therefore I have women of almost every ethnicity and age. My clientele varies in age range from the age of 21 and up. I match them according to preferences, age, ethnicity and according to the interest of the client - their knowledge on certain topics and various subjects. I hold standard because I would like to present the best in order to get compensated greatly, which I do.

Poppie

After Shayla and I got our ass beat by Tanya and Stephanie, I was not looking to get it beat the entire night. The crowd wound down and a few people left, which meant the level of the party was about to go up. It was all about the stay and play part of the party.

Austin stuck around and was eyeing me the entire time I was getting my ass beat in Spades. I had had enough and I was ready to have a nice, interactive conversation with Austin. He was looking all kinds of handsome standing next to the speaker near the wall.

He wore a nice, black track suit that fit him well against his butter pecan skin. I loved the way he smiled and licked his lips when he talked. After Shayla finally gave up the game, I sauntered over to Austin to get things started.

"Hey wassup," I said as I approached him close to his ear so he could hear me speak over the music.

"Hey, you done with the game?" he asked, hoping I'd say yes.

"Yup, done."

"C'mon," he said as he took my hand and led me up the stairs away from prying eyes.

As we stepped closer to the higher level, the sound of the music began to soften. He looked around for a room to choose to which I took his hand and led him into the spare room I had used before. I knew there was a lock on the door so we wouldn't be disturbed.

I locked the door behind us and turned on some twinkle lights I had installed the last time I was here. I had to crash here one night and I didn't want the light on as it was bright as fuck because she had a lamp with no shade sitting on the night stand. So Shayla had some twinkle lights she swiped from her Aunt's house and put them in the room for me.

"So now that you have me. What will you do to me?"

"Do to you? Or do for you?"

Interesting answer.

"Hmmm," I thought, not what I expected. "What will you do for me then?"

"Have you ever heard of a silent scream?"

"A silent scream?"

"Yes."

"No, I haven't. What is it?"

He stepped closer to me. I could smell his cologne. I could smell his scent. It makes my tulips quiver. He leaned in next to my ear.

I could feel his breath against my ear.

"You wanna find out?" he whispered softly and seductively. Curiosity traveled throughout my body so fast, I had the answer on my lips as I looked at him to respond.

He was so close, his lips were so full and wanting.

"Yes," I said looking at his bottom lip, wanting to suck it between my lips. He smiled as I looked up; his green eyes sucked me in as I stared deeply into them.

He moved his hand around to the small of my back and pulled me close as he held the back of my head. He slowly hovered over my lips, slowly licking them one at a time. We gazed at each other as he placed his lips over mine. His lips were soft and juicy.

He kissed me deeply, as I offered his tongue a dance with mine. His hand quickly found my ass and he grabbed a handful. My juices started to stir and boil as I was getting ready to have some fun with Mr. Austin.

He slowed his kissing to small pecks as he went down my neck and began to nibble. I unzipped his jacket and ran my fingers across his bare chest. I felt the heat inside his jacket as it brought the scent of him across my nose.

He had made his way down to my breast where he kissed them as I managed to help myself to sizing up his member. I pulled his pants down a bit and pulled out his soldier.

"Damn girl, you did that shit fast as fuck."

"Well I want you to be nice and ready so we both can enjoy this." I said as I began slowly stroking his shaft.

"Mmmmmhhhhmm," he said, as he leaned his head back down to my chest. He reached around and untied my halter top and the twins were free.

He flipped my halter up and took hold of them. He rolled my nipples between his fingers as they hardened with pleasure. I creamed a little as he watched me squirm as he pinched a little harder which made me stroke a little faster.

"Mmmmmm," I moaned as he took one into his mouth, sucking it profusely. I closed my eyes as I felt his tongue circle my nipple, then nibble it between his teeth. A spark hit my clit. He slid his hand down my underwear and between my lips.

He moved his fingers in a circle motion that made my mouth suddenly open; he filled my mouth with his tongue and kissed me hard.

I wanted this motherfucker and I wanted him now. I opened my legs and he slipped a finger in my cavern and I could hear the gush of nectar fill his hand as he moved it in and out.

"Uuuuhhhh......uuuuhhhh,.....mmmmmhhhh..." I moaned as the more he finger fucked me the more sloppy it became.

"Damn baby, you're so wet."

"Yeah, you got me dripping." He removed his fingers and licked them.

"Mmmm, sweet too." I smiled as this motherfucker was freaky as shit.

He quickly turned me around, raised up my skirt and pulled my panties to my ankles. He bent me over the bed and spread my legs. He grabbed my ass and took a long lick from my clit to my vajayjay.

"Oooooo, shit baby."

"Shhhhh. Silence," he mumbled. I don't know if a Bitch could keep quiet with what his tongue was doing to my insides.

"Uuuuuuhhh...Uuuuuhhh," I softly moaned. He continued licking me deeply inside as I could feel his tongue wiggle between my fleshy folds. His lips would suck away the wetness just after his tasting.

"Damn girl, your pussy is so sweet," he said as he stood up and wrapped his arm around my waist and pulled me back against him.

I felt the head of his cock, slide between my velvet walls as he fit snugly inside my cavern. He was bigger than I had expected as his length was way underestimated. He filled me completely.

"Oooo shit baby, you're shit is big," I said bracing myself as he slowly stroked in and out of my love nest.

"You think you can handle it?" he said, stopping.

"I can handle anything you got baby," I said with confidence while gripping the bed sheets in front of me.

"Okay baby, let me teach you about the silent scream," he said, grabbing my wrists and pulling it back.

He wrapped his arm around my waist and held me up as he covered my mouth and rammed himself deep inside my garden.

"Hmmmpphhff," I couldn't speak. He rammed me so hard, no sound came out, just air. It felt so fucking good. I screamed in silence and clinched my satin walls each time he entered; I let out nothing. it felt so good each time he went deep inside me, it made me want to scream.

I laid back against him with my arms dangling across his shoulders, holding onto his neck with my back arched as he fucked me from behind, increasing his speed about every third fuck. He grunted as he held onto my shoulders, pounding and thrusting forcefully in and out my wet pussy.

I could hear my juices sloshing around each time he entered and exited. Each time he entered, he would touch my spot. He hit it so hard and went so deep, a pain would ache deep inside me which sent a chill down my spine. My nipples instantly hardened to the point they ached.

He pounded me from the back, holding on to my ass from the back along with my skirt to keep the leverage. My eyes rolled back as my mouth stayed agape as he fucked me deep and hard as he bent his knees to slide in and out from damn near underneath.

He quickly pulled out from deep inside me and turned me around as I stood in a daze, my nectar dripping down my legs.

"Lay down and spread 'em," he said whispering to me. I followed my orders and laid on my back and spread my legs as wide as I could.

"Let me feel you," I said, beckoning him to enter. He stood before me stroking himself as I held on to my toes, holding my legs open waiting for him to land on my landing strip.

He dragged his head between my lips and across my clit. I threw my head back as he was driving me crazy. My pussy started pulsing, anticipating his entry. He slid it over and over, back and forth as my juice oozed out my honey pot.

He leaned down and kissed me hard as he rammed himself deep inside me. I wanted to scream. It felt so good as he covered his mouth with mine, demanding me not to make a sound. He held my thighs open as he watched himself slide easily in and out my pussy. Each time he exited, his shaft would be covered with my clear nectar.

I watched it become stringy as it started getting thicker. I was getting ready to cum hard. He noticed the change too and started ramming his dick deep inside me. His balls slapped against my asshole the faster he fucked.

"Uuuhhh...Uuuuu.. Uuuhhhh.," he huffed as he gyrated his hips, pushing his member deeper inside my cavern.

"Fuuuuuuuuuuu.....," I moaned as he covered my mouth. I was cumming and cumming hard. I wiggled beneath him as my white, thick cum covered his entire shaft. I started shaking as he was still fucking me harder as he was about to shoot his load.

"Uuuuuuugggggg....," he moaned as I covered his mouth. He closed his eyes as I felt his dick pulsating inside me releasing his warm jism.

He collapsed on top of me just as someone knocked at the door. They tried the handle but the door was locked so they got the picture and went elsewhere.

Austin released himself from me and rolled on the bed next to me. I sat up and grabbed a towel from the chair. I wiped myself clean and handed it to Austin. He cleaned himself up as I found my panties and tied up my halter.

"Poppie," he said, looking at me.

"Yes?" I said walking over and standing in front of him.

"Girl, you know you something."

"I know." I smiled. He leaned down and kissed me softly and sweetly. He caressed my cheek and kissed my forehead.

"You're dangerous."

"I know that too."

"You staying here all night?"

"Depends, are you?" I asked in return. He smiled and kissed me again.

"No, I didn't plan on it. You wanna go with me, over to my hotel?"

"I don't mind, but there is a matter of payment first." I didn't forget. I may have had a good time, but a Bitch still got bills to pay.

"I ain't forgot. I got you. But I want you for the rest of the night," he said, making me blush.

"Well, make it worth my time." I said. I know my worth. I know my shit is good and this was just a taste. I could make a motherfucker get stuck if I wanted. He just don't know who he's fucking with.

"Cool," he said and grabbed his phone. "What's your cash app?"

"PoppieLuv123,"

Shortly after I received a cash app notification.

This motherfucker sent me $1000.00! I looked at him, shocked as fuck.

"I take it, that I have you for the rest of the night," he said, sounding satisfied.

"Yes, you do."

Yes motherfucker, you got me for the rest of the motherfucking night, I thought. Shit, he paid for the wake up morning sex too!

Chapter 4 - Shit Just Happens

Waking up in a different place was a welcomed feeling, anything was better than waking up in my rundown apartment. I either had to cover myself up from a roach or a mouse running across me in the middle of the night. It's not like it happened every night, just the fact that it happens is enough honestly.

And waking up next to a fine, ass man in a hotel room was absolutely fucking phenomenal. Ausitn turned over and slowly opened his eyes.

"Good Morning Beautiful," he said, smiling and rubbing his eyes. It was wonderful hearing a gorgeous man calling me beautiful. I made it believable.

"Morning," I said, turning towards him. "How did you sleep?"

"I slept well," he said, scooting over and wrapping his arms around me. "Don't think you leaving me this soon. You ain't about to dip out."

I smiled, he wanted me to hang out. "Nah, I'm good. I have nothing planned for today."

"A'ight, cool," he said before he planted a kiss on me.

He cuddled closer to me, both of us still naked. I could feel his soldier growing between us.

"So what you wanna do today?"

"You," he said bluntly. I turned and looked at him as he held my hand and laced my fingers with him.

"As you wish," I responded. He kissed me deeply and we started our morning round of sex.

Austin and I hung out a good portion of the time he was in town. He was in Chicago for about 2 weeks and we went everywhere together. He would pick me up from work and I would stay over to the hotel instead of going home. Good thing I didn't have a pet, it would have died.

After Austin flew back to Miami, Shayla had another 'Play Party'. I'm glad she had other people she could depend on because I got sick shortly after Austin left and I was in no shape to 'Play'. It was all good, I was financially straight, thanks to Austin

I guess it comes in handy to have a baller even if he was semi-pro. He made sure I had enough money so that I didn't have to participate in those parties for a while. He knew how I made my extra money, he didn't mind but yet he did in the long run. He was acting like he didn't want me to hook up with anyone but we weren't in that type of relationship and I don't do that bullshit long distance shit, that never works. Fuck that, if my guy ain't here, I can't be with him

Anyway, while I was down with what I was told was a version of Covid, Shayla and Mike held the parties. Everything was good from what Shayla was telling me, they were making some ends which meant Christmas would be good and New Years would be off the chain, but then - shit hit the fucking fan.

I was rudely awakened by banging on my door, like it was the cops trying to bust in my fucking door. I jumped out of bed, looking at a hot mess, grabbed my robe and went to the door.

"What the fuck?!" I said opening the door to Tanya and Stephanie.

'Poppie! Girl yo' ass need to answer the fucking phone." Tanya said walking into the apartment.

"Bitch, I have covid! What the fuck do I need to answer the fucking phone for?" I yelled back at her. Stephanie had stopped at the door and covered her mouth.

"Bitch, did you hear what she said? She got fucking covid!" Stephanie yelled at Tanya. Tanya spun around and looked at me, covering her mouth.

"Oh Shit, I forgot! Shit! Shit! Shit!"

"What the fuck is going on?" I said, grabbing a mask and putting it on my face. "There's masks in the box by the door." I said as I pointed towards the box sitting on the window sill.

"Bitch," Tanya said as she put on her mask and walked into the living room. "Mike and Shayla got busted!" My eyes grew big.

"What? How?"

"The house got raided. Apparently they had been watching Mike for a while when he would get his packages. They got some shit on him for real." Stephanie said as she sat down on the couch.

"What the fuck! Dude, are you fucking serious?"

"I wish I wasn't, but yep, they got hit up about an hour ago. We were on our way over and when we hit the block, cops were everywhere. They had people lined up out on the street, getting into the back of da wagon."

"Shit, that's fucked up. So they holding Shayla too?"

"Yeah, for now. They might let her go. Mike most likely will tell them it was all him so she could get out."

"Yeah, but she knew about all that shit going on. I think they had an undercover somewhere in the house letting them know about what was going on upstairs too."

"You think?"

"Shit yeah, I would have thought you were a plant, but I've known you're light-skinned ass since you were little," she laughed. I shook my head. Damn, Shayla was locked up. I picked up my phone - I had a few missed calls from Austin. I'm sure he was trying to make sure I was okay and if I had heard about what happened to Shayla.

Just as I was about to put my phone down, it rang. It was Austin again.

"Hello?"

"Oh shit, good you are okay. I was worried about you. Did you hear what happened to Mike and Shayla?"

"Yeah, Tanya and Stephanie just came over and told me. I was knocked the fuck out."

"How are you feeling? I'm sorry I can't be there to take care of you."

"I'll be okay. I wish you were here too," I smiled at the fact that he wanted to take care of me.

"Well, let me call around and see what they are gonna face and I'll get back with you."

"A'ight cool," I said, putting the phone down. "That was Austin, he said he was gonna call around and see what charges they are gonna get."

"Shit, Mike's gonna stay for sure. He had so much shit in that motherfucking place it was ridiculous. You already know, Poppie." I did. I knew he had a lot of shit. He had a room upstairs just for his packages alone.

"Fuck!"

"Well, keep your phone close, just in case she calls you. We 'bout to go so we can find out if she's gonna get let out." Tanya said walking to the door.

"Okay, keep me posted." I said as they walked out the door.

Shit is fucked up. I was always worried about some shit like that, getting caught up with the cops and shit. I can't stand cops, they be shady as shit. Because I hang out with Black people and I may sound culturally different, they look at me as if I'm trash. It makes no sense how humans treat other humans. We all bleed red blood, but they don't give a fuck if you don't fit their 'standard'. You are considered a lost cause, a joke to society and looked upon as someone who basically has no say because I don't look, talk, or date the people they expect. People are people and they need to get the fuck over it.

This was the last thing I expected to happen with Shayla and Mike. I knew it was a possibility but I didn't expect it to happen honestly. Wishful thinking I guess. Fuck! I thought, I hope Shayla is okay.

I laid back down with my phone next to me and fell back asleep. This fucking covid had me down because a Bitch did not wake up until the next day. My phone had died, thank goodness I had a personal leave from work due to Covid. I had to test negative before I could be offered any assignments. I was good, though I just needed to get better.

As soon as I connected my charger, I received all of the text messages and voicemails that I had received. I had received a message from Austin that he had something delivered for me. I opened my front door and there was a huge gift basket with fruits and goodies, balloons and a card. It was an Edible Arrangements basket. I picked it up and placed it on my table. This man was incredible.

I called him to thank him for the basket, but he didn't pick up. I figured he was busy, so I just left a message. I checked all of my messages, which were a bunch from Tanya asking me if I had heard from Shayla.

I took a chocolate covered strawberry from the basket and scrolled through my messages and calls. Then my phone rang, it was Tanya.

"Wassup?"

"So, Mike is getting charged with everything but they had Shayla on charges of having prostitutes, and saying their house was a *brothel* - whatever the fuck that is," she said sounding disgusted.

"That's just a whore house." I defined

"Oh,...well shit, that's what the Bitch had! But the girls weren't whores, Y'all was some classy bitches," she said, sounding angry.

"Well did they say they were keeping her?"

"Nah, they letting her out with a court date. Thing is she ain't got no place to go. My momma had to get her out of jail so Shayla is going to stay with my momma for a while.:

"Fuck! For real?" Damn, that put me in a bad spot. I mean, Austin gave me some money to hold me over, but it wasn't going to be enough to hold me over like that though. Shit, I was banking on making some ends so I could get out of this place. Shayla was gonna help me with the deposit and shit, now I everything is fucked.

"Yup. She coming to get her and then they driving back to Texas in the morning." Tanya said, sounding disappointed.

"Damn, I wish she didn't have to leave, but I ain't got no place for her to stay either. I barely got a place for me."

"I feel you on that Sistah. Shit, well I figured I would let you know what went down and I'll holla at you later."

"A'ight, later." I said hanging up the phone. Shit, my girl leaving me and going to Texas of all places. You can't even smoke weed in Texas, that shit ain't even legal.

Chapter 5 - It Takes Two

Poppie

I don't know what the fuck happened with Austin but when shit hit the fan with Mike and Shayla, things started changing between Austin and I. Normally, he would call me in the mornings before I had to work when he was going to workout. It was nice to hear from him regularly. It made me smile knowing someone wanted to talk to me at the beginning of their day.

Austin would video call me at night before I went to bed; he would want to know how my day went and shit. He made me feel like someone really wanted me for me. But then the shit happened with Mike and Shayla and Austin became withdrawn. Slowly the morning calls started to decrease to the point, I went an entire week without getting a call from him.

I called him and he would answer sometimes, but he was always about to start practice, about to join a game or he was about to go to bed. Other times, the phone would just ring. I said fuck it after a few weeks, I got the fucking hint. He wanted to distance himself from his cousin and anybody associated with them. That's cool, it was good while it lasted, but the fucking money is almost out now.

Without those parties, I needed to find a way to come up with some extra cash in order to keep the heat and lights on because my temp job barely pays the rent. I had to use a nice chunk of change I had from Austin to pay my shit when I got sick with covid. A temp job has no sick time so, no work - no pay. I was out for a while which I was happy I had the extra money but after that I was fucked because I didn't have a back up.

Months had gone by since I had spoken to Shayla. I would see Tanya and Stephanie every once in a while but I ain't never really hung out with them without Shayla. Shit was starting to get tight and I had to make decisions I hadn't planned on.

I decided to have a few hook ups on the side with a few guys I had hooked up with before. Actually, I had taken it a step further and started to hook up with friends of hook ups. I hated the fact that I needed the money so desperately that I hadn't a choice.

I had a hook up tonight at a motel off of Stoney Island. I'm sure it's some shit hole, but it's enough to fuck and get paid so I could move on with my shit. I had to prepare myself before I went to the motel. From the text message, it was a guy I had hooked up with previously at the house.

I remember he liked to fuck quick, like a fucking jackhammer. He climaxed quickly and we had to go again, but he paid for both times so I took his number to hook up at another time. When I hit him up, he had a friend with him and asked if he could join. I usually don't do two at the same time but it was double the money and a Bitch needed money.

I told him his friend could come along as long as they sent the money; $200 now and $200 when I arrived. As I waited for payment, I decided to roll a nice blunt. I pulled out a small container out of my swivel table; it contained tabs of acid.

I wanted to be numb. I didn't want to feel anything they were about to do to me. I smoked half of the blunt by the time the payment came.

"Finally," I said as I pulled my hair into a ponytail and grabbed my pullover hoodie. This was just a simple fuck so there was no need to get dressed like I was going to the club - I was meeting these motherfuckers at a motel. Sweatpants and a hoodie was enough. I popped a tab of acid underneath my tongue as I waited for the Uber to pick me up.

The car ride wasn't a long ride from 119th and Parnell over to Skyway Motel, but it was long enough for the acid to take effect. The Uber pulled up in front of the hotel and I got out. They had texted me the room number so I walked over and knocked on the door.

"Hey wassup, Poppie," he said, opening the door with a smile. As I looked at him again, I remembered him. He was a cutie with dimples. He looked similar to Bow Wow, in height and build. He even had the light, hazel eyes to match.

"Hey Marcus," I said, giving him a hug after he closed the door.

"We got drinks and shit over there," he said pointing to a lone, circle table with two chairs. There were bottles of tequila, vodka and rum, along with a case of Heineken, juices and red plastic cups. They had planned a night for me, I'm glad they had refreshments.

"Okay cool," I said, going over to make myself a drink so I wouldn't feel a damn thing. "Y'all got weed?"

"Yeah, he's rolling up right now," Marcus said as he flipped channels on the tv. "Hey, this is Tony," he said, introducing us. I looked over and recognized this motherfucker instantly - as he did me.

"Snowbunny," he said, smiling as he rolled the blunt.

"John Legend," I retorted. Marcus laughed at my reply.

"Damn man, you do look like John Legend though," he laughed.

"How you been doing Tony?"

"I've been doing good, you?"

"Can't complain," I said as I poured at least two shots of vodka in a plastic cup. I followed it up with orange juice with a splash of pineapple juice.

"How long y'all plannin' on staying here?" I said looking at all the shit they brought to the hotel.

"Well, we was trying to play with you for a while. But we got some hoes coming too," he said as he lit one of the many blunts that laid on the side table.

"Oh a'ight, well why y'all call me if y'all got other bitches coming?"

"Cuz we 'bout to have a party up in here. We got other niggas and bitches coming after we finish with you," he said passing the blunt over to Tony.

"Shit, y'all still tryna have them 'Play parties', huh?"

"Yeah, we tryna keep that shit going 'til Mike get out."

"You know he gonna be in there a minute right?" I said as I took off my hoodie. I had a long sleeve, see-thru shirt with a hot pink, satin bra underneath. They weren't ready for me.

"Damn Snowflake, you look good as fuck," Tony said blowing out smoke.

"Thank you," I said, taking the blunt from Tony.

"Yeah I know they got him for a minute. Shayla out, but I don't know where she at though,"

"Wait, I thought she was supposed to stay with her Aunt in Texas?"

"She was until she got into a fight with her and she put her out. So I don't know where she at now," Marcus stated.

That's fucked up, no wonder I hadn't heard from Shayla. She ain't got no place to stay. Shit if I would've known that shit was gonna go down like that, I would have had her struggle with me, at least we would be together. Now I don't know where her ass is. I instantly felt lost.

I chugged my drink as I was floating sitting next to Tony. My body felt numb as my nipples were budding through my satin bra.

"You want another drink?" Tony said, pointing to my cup.

"Yeah, I'll get it."

"I'll get it, I'm getting me one too. Whatchu' have?"

"Vodka and OJ."

Tony brought my drink back and sat down closer to me on the couch.

"So Poppie, how you feelin'?" he said, taking a sip of his drink.

"I'm feelin' good, how you?" I took a few huge gulps. I wanted to feel fuzzy to deal with the shit I was about to do.

"You tell me," he said, taking my hand and putting it on his crotch. I could feel his dick move underneath my touch.

"You ready huh?" I said, looking at him.

"Yeah, I've been thinking about you since Marcus told me you was coming through," he said, turning towards me, handing me yet another blunt.

"Well, we have an issue. I didn't receive a payment," I said. I was straight up; no pay, no play. "Y'all forgot something."

"Fuck man, you didn't send her the rest of the money?" Tony said, turning to Marcus who was snorting a line of coke from the side table.

"Shit, I forgot," he said, grabbing his phone. "How much was it?"

"$300." I stated. I lied but figured if they ain't paying attention, it ain't my fault. Tony looked at me as I grabbed my phone. I needed confirmation before anything went down.

I received my cash app notification that I had received $400 from Marcus The Fly Guy. I looked over and he winked at me, I smiled because he knew the deal.

"We good?" Tony asked, trying to look at my phone.

"We good." I said putting my phone back in my hoodie pocket.

"Cool," he said, moving closer to me. He smelled really good but just a bit too much, he smelled like he poured the whole entire bottle on him.

He had a low cut fade with a low beard, tapered just right. Tony had deep brown eyes with long eyelashes that were so dark it looked as if he had on eyeliner. It made his eyes look sexy as he had the sleepy-eye look. He was just high as fuck; I didn't know they had coke until I saw Marcus take line. They were really planning to party.

Tony leaned over and kissed my neck, which sent chills down my spine. His tongue softly licked circles on my neck before taking a nibble. My nipples hardened by the feeling he was giving me. He leaned back and took the blunt from Marcus as Marcus joined us on the couch, sitting opposite from Tony.

Tony inhaled on the blunt and turned to me. He poked out his lips for me to inhale the smoke. I opened my mouth and inhaled as he blew into my mouth. He covered his mouth sloppily with his as he kissed me hard. I exhaled the smoke out my nose as he filled my mouth with his tongue.

It was like I was having an out of body experience. It was as if I was sitting on the bed watching the beginning of a threesome. I sucked on Tony's tongue as I felt Marcus grab my titties from behind. This shit was happening fast - the faster the better to be honest. I wanted this shit to be over with.

Marcus forcefully squeezed my titties and pinched my nipples. A chill went down my spine which made me arch my back, laying against him. Marcus bit and sucked my neck as Tony lifted my bra and let my twins loose. He sucked one hard and squeezed the other. I had hands all over my body at once I couldn't tell who's hand was whose.

I became submissive to them and allowed them to take control. Marcus lifted my shirt and unhooked my bra so I wouldn't be restricted. He stood up and removed his shirt and jeans and laid them on the chair. He laid down on the bed with his dick sticking through his boxers, stroking it slowly as he watched Tony suck and lick on my breasts on the couch.

"Hold on a minute," Tony said as he got up and removed his shoes, shirt and jeans and laid them on the other arm of the chair. He went over to the side table and drew two lines.

As he took the lines, I removed my jogging pants to reveal a hot pink satin thong that matched my bra. I stood there watching Tony take lines and Marcus stroking his dick. I took down the last of my drink in a few gulps and I hit the blunt real quick before I started on Marcus.

He was on the bed watching and stroking as I walked over to the side of the bed. He reached up and grabbed my tit and massaged it as I took hold of his shaft.

"It's been a while," he said, looking at me.

"Yeah it has." I said slowly picking up a rhythm.

I leaned down to his tip and licked his head across the top. He squirmed as he put his arms behind his head so he could watch me give him head. I closed my eyes and licked around his head, sucking his pre-cum out the hole. I slowly took his cock into my mouth, parting my lips slightly as I stroked him in.

"Oooooo...shit...babygirl..," he moaned lowly.

I took him in my mouth, sucking more and more the further I took him in. Tony had finally gotten himself together and was stroking his dick as he walked over to the bed. While I bent over Marcus giving him head, Tony came up behind me and moved my thong to the side, spread my ass cheeks and proceeded to eat my pussy from the back.

"Mmmmm...mmmm..," I moaned slowly as I took Marcus in and out my mouth.

"Damn girl, you got a juicy pussy," Tony said as he sucked away my juices. He was kneeling down, spreading my legs a bit more so he could bury his face in my shit. His long ass tongue flicked my clit as he slipped a finger deep inside.

"Mmm...mmmm...mmm..," I moaned as I stroked Marcus to feel the pleasure Tony was giving to my pussy. I could feel the wetness increasing between my legs.

"Fuck babygirl come here," Marcus said as he moved over on the bed for me to lay down.

Tony took a break from eating my deliciousness to remove my thong. I laid down on my back and opened my legs to allow easy access to Tony as he returned to eating my pussy. He circled my clit with his thumb as he slid two fingers deep inside me. My legs shook as he started moving them in and out. He sucked my clit while he fucked me with his fingers.

"Aaahhh.....aaaaaa....aaaaa," I moaned as I stroked Marcus. I looked at him and he crawled over, placing a kiss on my lips before bringing his dick to my mouth.

I sucked his thick dick between my lips as I fondled his balls

"Shit, babygirl, you wild," he said as he watched me take him in my mouth. He held my head as he started pumping in and out my mouth.

"I wanna feel that," Tony said as he slowed kissing my fleshy folds. He pulled his fingers out and sucked my nectar from them. He walked up to the side of the bed and put my dick in his hand. I sucked Marcus and stroked Tony's hardness as Tony reached down and played with my clit.

I squirmed as he rubbed my clit which made my juices start to flow. Marcus pinched and slapped my titties as I sucked him. I popped his dick out my mouth and replaced it with Tony's dick. His hard member was slender and smooth. It was hard as a fucking rock as he held my face and fucked my mouth.

"Gargh, gargh, gargh," I moaned as my spit sloshed around my mouth as he continued to fuck it in and out.

"Fuck this, I want that pussy," Marcus said moving over between my legs. He held them open while he put on a condom that he grabbed from the other night stand. I didn't even notice that they had a shit ton of condoms waiting to be used.

Marcus rolled a condom on his hardness and assumed the position. Tony was now fucking my mouth faster to the point, tears were coming out my eyes.

Was I crying? I couldn't tell. I didn't care. I needed this money to survive. I closed my eyes and let him fuck my mouth with spit flowing out the sides of my mouth; his dick glistening as he rammed my mouth in and out.

Marcus slammed his dick deep inside me and began to fuck me hard. He was pounding my pussy while I could hear my wetness squish as he moved in and out.

"Umm...Uuuhhh...Uhhhhh....Yes....this...pussy....feel....gooood...," Marcus moaned as he fucked me deep inside my cavern. He was hitting my spot and made me cream with each stroke. I was numb. I felt as if I was watching myself get fucked because everything felt so light.

I know I was stimulated, my pussy was soaked and my nipples were hard but it felt as if I was not getting the full effect.

"Shiiiit....suck it...take it all..," Tony said as he fucked my mouth. Marcus was fucking the shit out of me; I could hear my wetness sloshing upon contact.

"Ahhh, fuck...pussy....feel...so...good...," he said as he slowed up pounding me and started grinding his dick deep inside me.

"Fuck dude, flip her ass over, I wanna hit it," Tony said as he fucked my mouth and slapped my cheek. I didn't react to him slapping me. That was basic and expected. He pinched and slapped my tits as I sucked him down my throat. "Aaaahhhhh, fuck....suck this dick mama," he moaned.

After I released Tony from my mouth, I wrapped my legs around Marcus's waist and he flipped me over, me landing on top of him and him still deep inside. He held onto me tightly by wrapping his arms around my waist and started fucking me from underneath.

"Aaahh...Aaahh...Aaaaahhh.....aaaaahhh......ooooo,   shit fuck me baby," I said as I could feel his dick deep inside me. I held my tits close to his mouth so he could suck my nipples why he fucked me hard. It felt good at least from what I could feel. My body was tingling and feeling everything all of a sudden. Pleasure was running through me with each stroke. Tony finally returned after retrieving a condom from the table.

Suddenly, I felt my ass cheeks spread with a cold liquid being dropped. Tony had gotten some lube and poured on my ass and some on his dick. I could hear the suction between Marcus and I as we fucked in sync. Tony slowly slipped a finger in my ass and it made my back arch. It had been a while since I had taken a dick in the ass, but there was no going back today. I needed this money so, I needed to take this dick.

My pussy pulsates around Marcus's dick deep inside me as we slow down to allow Tony to join the party. I started grinding my pussy against Marcus as he slapped me again.

"Fuck that shit bitch, you know," he moaned loudly. My face stung as I could feel the heat growing where he made contact.

"Uhhhh....Uhhhhh.....Uhhhhh......Yess.....fucck me....ffffuuuuuccckk...," I moaned with ecstasy.

Tony finally joined us and mounted me as he slid his dick slowly in my ass. I could feel the walls of my ass being stretched the more he pushed. I clutched the sheets as I braced for entry.

Pain ached as he continued to push his head deep in my ass. Tears started to fall as Marcus grabbed my throat. I could feel the pressure of having two dicks inside me at once.

Tony started to fuck my ass slow as he readjusted himself over me and Marcus. As he got a better footing, he began to fuck me slow and deep.

"Aaah....aaaaahhhh ... .aaaaahhh.....aaaahhhh...," I moaned with my eyes closed while Tony was holding onto my hips from the back.

The guys picked up speed as they pounded deep inside me, we found a collective rhythm. As my pussy went down on Marcus's shaft, my ass went up on Tony's throbbing hard cock.

"Fuck...this....shit...," Tony said as he started banging in my ass. Pain increased as he was banging deep inside, but I didn't care, it was almost over. Tony slapped my ass cheeks as he pounded me.

"Uhhh...Uhhhh...Uhhhh....Uhhhh...," I moaned as Marcus grabbed my twins and sucked both nipples in his mouth as we rocked back and forth on the bed.

"Shhhhh......fuuuuu....I......Ima....Ima...," Marcus stuttered as his eyes rolled back. I could feel his dick harden deep inside my pussy, he was about to shoot his load.

"Uhhh....Uuuhhhh....Uuuuuhhhh....fuck...mmeee....pleeaasssseeee I loudly moaned as I reached my climax which triggered both of them to reach theirs. My pussy started pulsating as both of them began to pound me harder and harder just before they shot their load. I could hear the wetness of my pussy as I came hard all over Marcus's dick.

"Fffffffuuuuuuuuuuuuucccccccckkkkkkkkkk!" Marcus yelled as he shot his load first. I could feel his warm liquid fill the condom deep inside my pussy.

"Taaaakkkkkeeee.....this....ssssshhhhh iiiiiiiiiii tttttttt!" Tony finally shot his load as he rammed deep inside my ass. I collapsed on top of Marcus as Tony released himself from my ass and laid down on the extra bed. His dick was still pulsating as he removed the cum-filled condom, tied a knot and threw it on the floor.

I rolled off Marcus, with his arms still around me. I laid next to him in his arms.

"You good babygirl?" Marcus asked, looking at me. It was nice that he wanted to know if I was okay. He moved a few strings of hair from my face that had come from my ponytail.

"Yeah, I'm good. Tired but good."

"Good. You staying? You don't have to play, if you don't want but you know you can stay and drink and smoke," he offered. The thought was good, as I didn't have anything planned for the rest of the night. I had done what I came to do, so I was good to go.

"I'll see. I might stay a lil bit." I said looking at him.

"A'ight cool," he said, smiling at me. He leaned over and kissed me on the forehead. He slid off the bed, removed his condom and dropped it in the trash. I finally moved off the bed, grabbed my clothes and went to the bathroom to freshen up.

In the bathroom, I looked at my reflection in the mirror. I could see the redness on my face where Marcus slapped me a couple times and a few red marks on my neck, from him choking me. Rough sex goes with the territory, so it was something I had gotten used to.

As I came out of the bathroom, they guys were fully dressed. Marcus had turned on a bluetooth speaker that had Doja Cat singing *Juicy*, and they had started back smoking the blunts. Hell I didn't want to spend my hard earned money on smoke and they had a nice supply so I figured I would stay and at least smoke. I missed Shayla. Not sure if I'll play again, but I'll definitely smoke and drink.

I thought about it after a while. If the right guy had the right pay, I just might play - a bitch still has bills.

Chapter 6 - Rock Bottom

The party started jumping and I knew I should have left before everyone started showing up. The room was packed with guys and chicks wall to wall. Smoke filled the air so thick a person would swear that something was on fire somewhere.

I hung out with Marcus for a bit, sitting on his lap while he played Spades, I was just there to smoke the blunts that were going around. I was feeling lifted as I kept refilling my drink to the point I wasn't adding any mixer, it was just alcohol. *Straight vodka.* I was talking softly with Marcus when Tony passed him a plate with two lines of coke. Marcus inhaled a line quickly and pinched his nose. He sniffed his nose, looked at me and he offered the plate and waited for my response. I should have said no, but my stupid ass didn't and I did the line.

My nose burned crazy hot, then I sniffed again hoping it would subside soon. I closed my eyes and pinched my nose mimicking Marcus. Marcus rubbed my back while he passed the plate back.

"You good?"

"Yeah, I'm good." At least, I thought I was. I wasn't. I was fucked up.

After a while, I was sitting next to Marcus, moving to the music and Marcus excused himself from the table. My eyes were barely open as I leaned against the wall waiting for Marcus to return. He was in the corner talking to two chicks that were looking back at me. I really didn't do anything about it and just shrugged it off. Marcus returned and leaned in to me.

"Hey Poppie," he spoke softly to me so as to not draw attention. "You wanna make an easy $500?"

"How easy?" I said sitting up. " Wait a minute, I don't know, I'm kinda tired." I just had two guys and I wasn't planning on a replay.

"Nah, you ain't gotta fuck no Niggas," he said. I looked at him strangely. "It's some Bitches that wanna get with you."

I looked at him to see if he was serious - he was.

"Who?" I asked and he pointed to two chicks sitting on the bed having a moment between themselves.

"Oh," I watched them as they kissed and caressed each other on the bed. Everyone was fucked up and to be honest, this was one of those 'freaky' parties so people didn't give a fuck.

E'erybody was doin' sum' of e'erythang, e'erywhere. Feel me?

"They said they wanted to get down with you, if you didn't mind. I told 'em you had a price tag."

"For real?"

"Yup. It's PoppieLuv123, right?"

"Yeah," I replied. He looked at me and apparently I gave him the go ahead and he went to provide them with my cash app ID. By the time he got back to the table, I received $500 from muffbuddy420.

The two girls were hot as fuck, neither one of them were 'Butch'; I figured I could get my pussy eaten correctly with passion from those who know exactly how to handle the vajayjay and know all the secrets hidden deep within. I walked over to the side of the bed and they invited me to join in - and for $500, I did.

My alarm had buzzed and woke me up, scaring the shit out of me to be honest. I looked at the clock, it read 9:35 am. SHIT! I overslept - AGAIN!

"FUCK!" I yelled as I jumped my ass out the bed and ran to the bathroom. I was supposed to be at the office at 8:30!

Ever since the party at the hotel, I have not kept my shit together. I had been hooking up with Marcus and his parties weekly since he had been hooking me up with some people who have been paying good money to keep my lights on. Yet lately, I've been struggling staying on top of shit like before. I was already on a temporary basis and on two write ups since the last party. I had one more chance before I would be shit canned.

Hanging out with Marcus has been a blessing and a curse as it gave me more money but I started a habit that I didn't expect to pick up. Since Marcus throws the parties and he has me involved, I get free access to weed and shit. So I'll do a couple lines with Marcus every now and then to help cope with shit. I still hadn't heard from Shayla and I don't know if she's alive or dead.

One day I went into work, high as fuck right directly from the hotel. I got sent home from the client and was immediately reassigned. My employment manager, Monica, at the agency told me that I was walking on thin ice and that I needed to have no attendance concerns for at least 2 months before I would be back to good standards.

Well I fucked that up. I looked at the mirror at my reflection. I didn't even look like myself. It looked like I hadn't slept in days, there were dark blueish circles underneath my eyes. My hair wasn't as silky as it is usually and I looked paler than pale. I looked like a goddamn ghost or even worse, I looked dead! I knew I was white but I was too fucking white!

Just then, my cell phone rang. I could hear it from the living room of my small apartment. The ringtone let me know it was my job calling me. I didn't want to answer it. I already knew what they were going to say. Fuck. Shit. Damn. I just shook my head and let it go to voicemail. I didn't even want to deal. I had another hook up set for later on and I needed the fucking money, especially since I knew they had fired me.

I didn't have to pick up the phone to know, I just had a feeling. I brushed my teeth and washed my face. I turned on the shower as hot as possible while I went to grab a change of clothes. On the way back, I played the voicemail that was left.

[Employment Manager] This message is for Penelope Matthews. This is Monica Andrews, the Manager at Employment Express. Could you please give me a call as soon as possible? Your assignment for today has been reassigned. Please call me at your earliest convenience.]

Yeah, I already knew that shit would happen. "Fuck!" I was mad at myself because this shit could have been avoided. I had no one to blame but myself. I took off my sleeping shirt and stepped into the shower, letting the hot water burn my skin turning it red. The pain felt so good sending chills through my entire body.

I let the water fall over my head as the water trickled down through my hair to flow down my face as I closed my eyes. The warmth of the water brought my skin back to life as I was struggling this morning. I needed to find another job as this temp shit ain't cutting it. I had overheard someone say that the Tootsie Roll factory was hiring. Shit, I need to get that job.

I would have to get my ass up extra early to make that work because I heard they have three shifts at the factory. I wanna work early so I can get that shit done and over with. I just need to stop fucking with Marcus and his parties.

The water saturated my hair as I smoothed my hair back, raised my head to allow the water spray on my face. I needed to get my shit together. I just need a come up and I need it now. I can see myself going down, slowly - but a steady decline.

After the shower, I wrapped myself with my robe and rolled a blunt before calling the agency. I figured if I was going to get fired, I might as well be in a good mood about it. I grabbed my wallet and pulled out a small baggie with a small amount of coke. Marcus gave me this to start my day. I poured the contents on the back of past due notice and made two lines. I did both quickly, pinched my nose, picked up the residue and spread it across my teeth. I was hooked, I knew it. I didn't want to be but it was the only 'friend' at the moment that I had to confide in.

I lit the blunt, picked up the phone and dialed the number.

"Hi, may I speak to Monica please?"

"Whom shall I tell her is calling?"

"Penelope Matthews," I answered and she put me on hold. I inhaled and blew out the smoke slowly, making circles in the air.

"Hold on while I transfer you," she quipped and immediately transferred the call.

"Penelope," Monica answered sternly.

"Hello,"

"Are you okay?"

"No, I'm not, if you want an honest answer. But I know I need this job," I said pleading my case, but not really.

"I understand you need the job but you need to show up for the job you need. I can't promise a client a temporary replacement who doesn't show up."

"I know, if you could just give me..,"

"You're out of chances Ms. Matthews. We discussed this the last time this happened. I don't know what is going on in your personal life, but it seems to be hindering you from completing assignments."

"I know, I've just had a few personal things happen, but I'm working on it,"

"That's what you said the last two times. I'm sorry, but it seems as though your personal matters do not allow you to meet our requirements. Therefore I am closing your contract with us. I'm sorry but we will no longer be contacting you for any future assignments. I wish you all the best in your future endeavors." she calmly said. I didn't know what to say. I had no rebuttal because she was telling the truth.

I was a liability for the company and she was right, she can't tell a client that she has someone who just doesn't show up. I really fucked up this time.

"I understand and I'm sorry for everything."

"I'm sorry too Ms. Matthews, have a good day." Monica said as she disconnected the call.

I just put the phone face down and pulled long on the blunt. I put my feet up on the cocktail table as I had nowhere to go since I was no longer employed. I really needed to show up for the hook up tonight because now, a Bitch *really* needs money.

Shayla

I hope I can find Poppie's ass. I had been hearing she had been out here slinging her shit for some ends and if that was the case, then I have an offer she can't refuse. The last thing I had heard was that Poppie had been hanging out with Marcus and she got hooked on the powder. She is so much better than that, but I know she was lost after left. I didn't have a choice. It was either stay in jail or go back with my Auntie who got me out of jail.

Only thing is, that shit didn't last long. She acted that since she paid for me to get out of jail that I was her live-in slave! This bitch had me doing every fucking thing around the house and a bitch didn't even work. I got tired of that shit after I was on my hands and knees cleaning that nasty ass, dirty floor and this bitch came walking in crossing the floor I just cleaned and mopped with muddy ass shoes because it was raining outside and she stepped in a mud puddle.

I lost it on that Bitch! I swung on her and she is glad I didn't make contact. My Aunt was talking out the side of her mouth thinking she was gonna treat me like that because she put up the money. She said had my mother been alive, she would have left me there. Shit to be honest, Auntie should have left me there if she was gonna act like that towards a member of the family.

I left about a month after I had moved in with her. Luckily I still had money from Mike, it wasn't a lot but it kept me until I got my ass back in Chicago. I ran into someone who helped me out in more ways than one and I wanted to get Poppie hooked up with her. After working for her for a few months, I have my own place, money saved in the bank, a wardrobe out of this world and I don't work a regular 9 to 5.

My Aunt was floored when I sent back her fucking bail money. I told the Bitch I don't want nothing else from and to lose my fucking number. Of course, the bitch is always trying to call me asking me for some money. I just ignore her calls and go about my day, I don't have time for the bullshit.

I heard that Poppie got fired from the temp agency. Word on the street is that she's been hanging out with Marcus having these 'play parties 'cause she needs money. I also heard she may be strung out as well. If that is true, I really need to find her because she needs to get clean in order to work.

It was early in the morning by the time I reached Poppie's apartment. If she ain't got a job, then she should be at home, I thought. I walked up the steps and rang her doorbell. I could hear her coming down the stairs to open the door.

"Who the fuck is it?" she yelled from behind the door.

"Bitch, open the fucking door, it's cold out here!"

Instantly, I heard locks being unbolted and the door knob turn. Poppie opened the door looking fucked up - she looked fucking tired.

"Shayla!" she screamed.

"Poppie!" I yelled in return. We grabbed each other and held on tightly.

"Bitch, where you been?" she said, stepping out the way to let me in the door. She closed and locked the door and we went upstairs to her apartment.

"Bitch, I've been here actually. I was taking care of my shit so I could come and get you."

"What you mean? Come and get me?"

"I heard you lost your job."

"Oh damn, that shit just happened like 3 hrs ago, how the fuck..,"

"Monica called me. She had been keeping an eye on you for me."

"So she knew where you were all this time?" she said, sounding as if she was getting pissed off.

"No, she was just letting me know how you were doing since I had left."

"Oh," she said, lighting up a blunt. "So where you been?"

"Well, it's complicated but rewarding. I don't know how to explain it."

"So you staying in Chicago?"

"Yep, I got myself an apartment in Lincoln Park."

"Lincoln Park! How you swing that?"

"That's what I wanted to talk to you about. You need to get clean." I said. She knew what I meant. She knew I had my ways of finding out.

"I know," she said, pulling on the blunt and passing it over to me. "I hadn't even planned on starting, now I gotta get off this shit."

"Well in order for me to bring you in with me, you need to get clean. Weed is okay, but you gotta get off any other shit you are on, for real." I said pulling on the blunt. It was nice to be back smoking with my girl.

"Okay, what you got a job for me?"

"A good job that has hella benefits."

"For real, how much it pay?" she said, trying to see if it was worth it.

"I get 2 grand a night." I said and watched her eyes get big in her head.

"2 Gs for real? What the fuck do you do?"

"I go on dates."

"Dates?"

"Yes, and it's more if sex is involved."

"What?" she answered. I knew she was confused but everything will make sense later.

"I'll tell you more about it, but you definitely need to get off the coke."

"Yeah," she said as she took the blunt and pulled on it. "Well, I did two lines today. That was the last of my shit. I got a hook up tonight though."

"Cancel it. You're coming with me."

"Cancel? Bitch I have no money. I'm behind in rent and I barely kept the light on in this motherfucker last month."

"Bitch, cancel the hook up. You are moving in with me. I need you clean so you can be my partner in crime again. We're gonna do this shit legit and make bank."

"Moving with you?" she said, looking at me. "Are you serious?"

"Yup, pack yo' shit." I said as I took the blunt from her and puffed on it. I blew the smoke in her face as she looked at me. "Go. get. yo'. shit. I'll wait."

Chapter 7 - On the Come Up

Shayla

I finally got Poppie over to my apartment and set her up in the extra bedroom. I intentionally decided to get a 2 bedroom, so I could find Poppie and help her out. We have been through a lot together and I know she was struggling when I left. I was like her protector, I took care of her when we were in the facility because all we had was each other. She was like my sister.

The first week of detox was hard for Poppie as she went through a lot of shit getting off the cocaine fix. Within the first day, which was the day I found her, she informed me that she had just taken two lines. I didn't see any need to wait for her to detox so we started shortly after she moved in.

Poppie started experiencing withdrawals within a few hours after her last hit. I had taken a personal leave, so I had the next few days off to help her get back on her feet. At times, Poppie was exhausted and sweating so much, she would get pissed off at me because I wouldn't turn on the air conditioning. If she wasn't throwing up she would sit up for hours walking around the apartment because she was sleep deprived. Poppie went through so many withdrawal symptoms I didn't know if she would make it - she was going through it *bad*.

She had tremors, convulsions and even hallucinations. She looked like she was dying right in front of me. She *spaced out* at times that I had to check on her to see if she was still breathing. I cried for her because she was in so much pain and discomfort, I didn't know what to do. I couldn't take it away and I felt horrible. It had gotten so bad, that I found myself praying to God that she would wake up the next day feeling just a little bit better.

Seven days went by and Poppie emerged from the bedroom one night as I was watching tv one night.

"Hey," Poppie said as he walked into the living room.

"Hey girl, how you feelin'"

"Like shit," she said, flopping down on the couch wrapped in a huge, fleece, hooded robe. She wrapped it tightly around her and sat with her legs folded in front of her.

"Well, you had me worried for a few days, but it's good to see you on the other side," I said, looking over at her and smiling.

"Thank you girl," she said as she sniffed. "I....really...,"

"I know," I interrupted her. "I got you." Poppie smiled a weak smile. She was almost 100% but not quite there yet. I wanted her to be at her best because I knew she would do well.

"Thanks,"

"You hungry?" I asked.

"Yeah,"

"You wanna smoke?" I asked, passing her the blunt I had rolled on the table. "It might help with your appetite."

"You're right," she said as she took it and lit the end. She inhaled the smoke and closed her eyes to let it resonate in her soul. She had missed it. I knew she did.

"Weed only, okay?" I reminded her.

"Yeah, I got it." I handed her the ashtray and went to grab her a bite to eat.

I had ordered a Giordano's Pizza which we both loved. It's been a while since Poppie's had one I'm sure. It feels good to be able to give it to her when she needs sustenance.

"Ooooo Shit, Giordano's?" she said looking at the slice of deep dish pizza on the plate I was handing her. She reached for and held on to it as if it was her last meal.

"So," I started. I sat down on the couch, opposite of her. "I'd say next week I'll bring you in with me to meet my boss."

"Your boss," she said with her mouth fairly full of food. "You got it like dat?"

"Yes," I said, handing her a paper towel. "I got it like that." I said pronouncing the 'th' which is part of the word.

"Oh, 'cuse me then Miss Thang," she said, waving her hand and holding her pinky in the air.

"I know I've changed a bit but for the better." I said, taking a sip of my drink. "But I can still be dat Bitch when I need ta be, ya feel me?" We giggled; it felt good to have her here with me.

"But for real though, what do you do?"

"I work for a very wonderful woman, named Vanessa McBride. She has helped me in so many ways, I can't even explain it," I said looking at her.

"That still ain't telling me what you do," Poppie stated rolling her eyes. She stabbed a piece of pizza stuffed in her mouth while waiting for me to respond.

"We were close Poppie, but we were nowhere near close to the level she is," I was right. Vanessa was in her entirely one realm.

"What the fuck are you talking about, Shayla?" Poppie said getting frustrated with me. I smiled and turned towards her.

"I met Vanessa the day I got bonded out of jail. To be honest, I should have left with her instead of my Aunt, had I known what my Aunt was going to do with me. I could have been on my own much earlier and I probably would have been able to get you sooner."

"Damn,"

"Right. Anyway, I met her when my Aunt had just paid my bail. Vanessa was in the waiting room when I was released. When I saw her I was like, why would a woman like her be in a place like this? She was dressed, Poppie. She was breathing money. She looked she dropped coins as she walked, just leaving change,"

"Damn, got so much money it just flows off of her huh?"

"Girl, if you only knew,"

"Bitch, I'm trying but yo' ass draggin a fuckin story man,"

"Chile please," I said, throwing a pillow at her. She caught it and giggled. "Okay shit, it's just that she saved me Poppie....she really did."

"Well let me in on it, shit,"

"She gave me her card that day. She told me that she knew about my record and that I had a good concept but I went about it all wrong. She told me if I ever wanted to know how to do it the right way then to give her a call"

"The right way to do what?"

"She knew I was hosting the Play Parties. She said she wanted me to bring me in and learn the ropes. I told her about my Aunt and she said when I was ready to let her know and she would take care of everything."

"Damn, who is this woman?" she asked.

"Vanessa McBride is the owner and CEO of Elegant Escorts and Illustrious Women."

"Okay?"

"She's also known as The Notorious Madame of Chicago,"

"Oh shit! For real?" Poppie said as her eyes got bulged out. She knew exactly who I was talking about.

Vanessa had a trial not long ago which made her known as the Madame of Chicago because she was accused of having a brothel or what some may call it, a 'whorehouse'. She beat the wrap because the prosecution couldn't get any of the charges to stick. Their case started to fall apart due to no evidence and those who were supposedly clients of Vanessa wouldn't go against her. The Bitch was Bad with a capital 'B'.

"Yup,"

"Wait, you work for her?"

"Yup and the shit is legit Poppie. It's not like what you think,"

"So you fuck guys for money, big money,"

"That's one way of thinking about it but not exactly. It's not all like that,"

"So fill me in," she said leaning in for a better understanding.

"Not all of its sex. We get paid to go on dates. And the dates are with distinguished men like politicians, business executives and international representatives,"

"International representatives? Are you serious? Politicians?"

"Yes. Vanessa makes sure we are totally schooled in what we need for any type of client and interaction that we may have during the date. Sex is extra,"

"You fucking me?"

"Not at all, straight truth Bitch,"

"Shit, we on the come up!"

"That's what I'm saying!"

"So what do I have to do?"

"Well, for starters you have to go to what is called 'Finishing School',"

"What the fuck?" she yelped. I giggled.

"I know right? I had the same reaction. But apparently, it was called that back in the day whereas women who were basically born into a rich family had to attend these classes to enhance their social graces and etiquette as well as cultural studies which will prepare them for social activities,"

"What the fuck?"

"Basically, the goal is to teach us how to be cultivated, educated and graceful. They teach us how to host, entertain, and socialize with the elite,"

"Oh shit," Poppie's mouth hung open. She couldn't believe what I had just said. I couldn't either, but I must admit, I learned a lot.

"Yeah,"

"Was it hard?"

"Nah, it's easy. We just gotta smooth off the rough edges. That's what Vanessa likes. She wants real women who are hungry to get theirs and work hard at getting it. She said a sophisticated and educated woman is a woman....shit, how did she say it? Um., "

"How to say sophisticated and educated?"

"No silly, she said a Sophisticated and Educated Woman is a woman who ought not be crossed. It won't end well."

"Damn,"

"She knows her business and there is no one like her. She said she admired that I tried to host parties and she wanted to show me the correct way,"

"Well fuck," Poppie said as she caught herself and covered her mouth. "Um, I guess we don't curse, huh?"

"We do, but when the time is appropriate. You will learn just like I did. It's not hard Poppie, I swear. Before you know it, you will be bringing in that cash and speaking three different languages." I said and she turned and looked at me.

"Bitch, you speak another language?"

"Si, Mamacita," I answered. Poppie squinted her eyes and looked at me.

"Bitch, you already know Spanish,"

"Oui, mon ami," I spoke in French.

"Well fuck me," she sat back and smiled. "Bitch, what you say?" I looked at her with my head tilted and the corners of my lips turned up. "Sorry, what did you just say?"

"I said, yes my friend,"

"Aw shit, yeah, I'm ready, I'm down. I wanna learn a new language. I want to learn Italian or Chinese or,"

"Mandarin is very hard to learn just so you know. It is possible, just hard," I responded.

"I don't want to learn Mandarin, I want to learn Chinese,"

"Mandarin is their language,"

"Oh, well yeah, fuck it, I want to learn it. I want to learn how to place my order at the chinese food restaurants," she said smiling. I just shook my head.

Poppie was always the one who made me smile. She might not be the smartest cookie but she had her moments.

"Well you just worry about getting better first and we'll start next week after you have your one on one with Vanessa,"

"One on one?" she said, sounding concerned.

"Yes, she meets with everyone one on one. It's okay, she doesn't bite. She just wants to get to know a bit about you and to learn your strengths and weakness so she and enhance what you have and grow what you don't,"

"Oh ok, if you say she's cool, then we're cool,"

"I'm sure she's going to love you Poppie, you're my girl. I've already told her so much about you. She knows that we were both in a facility together. She likes to bring in girls of a certain age, legal of course, and of different backgrounds and ethnicities so she can cater to those of her clientele,"

"Oh ok Vanessa,"

"Yep, she is on top of her shit for real,"

"So you really made 2 grand a date?"

"Yep, but it depends. It starts between $500 - $1000, that is the starting rate. As I told you it varies because it depends on the clients. But sexual dates will start at $1500 and can go up from there,"

"Shit!" Poppie fell back on the couch and looked up to the ceiling in disbelief. "Thank you for coming to get me, girl. I really appreciate it. I tried to hold on but...,"

"It's okay girl, that's why I had to get my shit together so I could help you get your shit together,"

"Cool, thanks."

"You're welcome girl. You my sistah for real. You know I love your light, bright ass," I said smiling while walking over to give her a hug. She opened her arms and we embraced each other.

"I love you too girl, I wouldn't have made it this far without you. You are the only people I got," Poppie said as I sat next to her. I held her hands looking at her fingers. She needed a manicure, badly.

"I know. You are the only family I care about. All them other niggas can kiss my black ass," I said and she smiled.

Poppie and I sat up and finished off another slice of pizza each and I opened a nice bottle of wine for us to enjoy. She wasn't ready for the wine but I told her I attended culinary classes and totally fucked her up when I bought out a charcuterie board with fruit, meats, cheeses and crackers. She seemed excited to get to my level and I wouldn't be surprised if Poppie excelled in all of her classes. As long as she keeps her shit together, smoke weed and her nose clean she will go far.

Chapter 8 - Lost and Found

Vanessa

Today is a normal yet stressful day for me. Today I will meet my ladies who will join my company. I have to make sure all of the contracts are signed and that their accommodations have been set.

"Mr. Peabody," I called from my walk-in closet. I looked at myself in the mirror to see how my outfit looked.

I must admit, I'm sure my father is rolling over in his grave just disgusted that I made it as a woman. I may have made it as a woman, but because of him, I can't value a love a man can give a woman because he never gave it to me or my mother.

I am a product of my father, I know exactly how he was. He fucked anything and everything that had tits, legs and a pussy. I remember when I caught him fucking the maid in the kitchen. He had his hand over her mouth as she was holding onto the counters. He was hitting it from the back and I thought - this is my father.

Then I looked at the girl that had no choice because she had a job and needed it. She knew the consequences of working for my family. My brothers were just like him. Word got around town quickly about my household. I knew why he didn't want me to go into the 'family business', because he didn't see value in women. He saw them as property to be used as he pleased.

As I looked for my shoes, Mr. Peabody appeared quietly. He looked so handsome to me. Dark skin that was smooth over his entire body. I love that he keeps himself in tip top shape as I do. He has been a good companion for me. I'm truly grateful for him.

"Yes Ms. McBride," he stood with his arms folded behind him, holding a tablet for any of my unexpected requests.

"Where are my shoes that go so well with this outfit?" I said strolling along the wall checking out the shoe compartments, carefully looking again.

"I believe those are returning today. The strap broke, I sent them in," I stopped looking and turned to him. I smiled and walked over to him .

He inhaled as I stood in front of him. Mr. Peabody. He has been so good to me, in so many ways. I touched his face and he inhaled my scent, turning his head to my hand and leaving a kiss on my palm.

"You know exactly what I need," I said slowly, caressing his face.

"That is my duty," he said, glancing directly at me.

"You're too good to me,"

"No Ma'am, not enough," he quipped, stepping forward. He was close to me. I could smell his cologne. It's the one I bought for his birthday.

It makes me want him. Now.

I lean in and kiss his lips softly and he pulls me to him. My tongue searches his mouth and dances with his. Our breathing mixes and we inhale each other's breaths. I feel his hand grope my ass as I kiss him deeply.

I suddenly stopped. I look at him and he understands. He straightens up and regains control. We have a job to do yet he caters to me at any and all times.

With whatever I need.

"Would you like for me to find another pair for you or would you like another outfit altogether?" he asked as he stepped back and folded his arms in front.

"Another pair is fine. I'll find them. I'm sure you have other things you have to take care of,"

"You come first," he said and made my heart melt.

"I know. But how are you? Are you good?" I asked. I wanted to know about him. He is human and he has his own goals and dreams.

"I'm good, thanks for asking," he smiled. He blushed. I loved his smile. I know it made him feel good when I asked about him.

He knows I care for him dearly. He cares for me too.

"Ok, so is everything set for today?" I asked as I looked again for a good pair of comfortable shoes to match my outfit.

"Yes Ma'am, we are set to bring on 5 girls," he said looking at his tablet. "Oh and we are supposed to get a direct referral from Shayla. Her friend is Penelope Matthews."

I instantly froze. I believe that was the name I was waiting to hear for such a long time, I was not sure if I would ever hear it.

"Uh, repeat that last name for me please?" I said bending down and grabbing a pair of Gucci straps from the lower level shelf.

"Uh, that was Penelope Matthews. Shayla was the one who referred her to you, Wait, is that?" He realized it too. I had him on lookout for that name.

"I believe we have found her," I said smiling as I fastened my shoes and walked over to the mirror. Perfect pairing.

"Wow," he said, walking over and standing behind me. "Do you think you really found her though?"

"I hope so," I really did. I had been looking for her for a while. I wasn't sure if I would find her in this way, but I had hoped indirectly so to speak.

"Well, I really want to see how this plays out," he said, smiling and shaking his head. He has his thoughts about the subject, but I have the final say. I am the boss.

"Well you will. Go ahead and take care that all the documents are ready for signature and confirm all of the accommodations," I said as I started waving him off. He took the hint and started backing away.

"Oh and don't forget to set up the classes after the meetings," I yelled as he walked out the room.

My ladies will have a lot to do when they come into this company. I want nothing but the best. That's why we have very strict guidelines in order to work for me. I worked hard for my shit and I will take down anyone who tries me. No questions asked. When the line is crossed, all bets are off and I come for blood.

I know the name they give me on the streets. I know what people say about me. I don't care. I run a business that is strategically stable. My ladies are paid well in doing what they do and every one is extremely satisfied. I learned from watching my father and how he treated the women who worked for my family.

I would think it was a shame that they had to do double duty, sometimes triple duty when my brothers were involved and didn't get paid extra. It was crazy. My mother didn't care because she had her own thing going on with the neighbor and his wife. My household was ridiculous.

All I knew was sex, sex and more sex. No love. That didn't exist in my house or my family.

So I grew a detachment to the word 'love' having never known the true meaning. I know *SEX* and what that entails. I know the passion it can bring between two people for a moment. I know it can intimately connect people to a point of unimaginable pleasure that you feel throughout your entire being.

I figured if the women who are subjected to the life of sex then why not get paid well for it and do it professionally? In the adult entertainment industry, women get paid to fuck more than the men. Therefore bring that same concept into a business that invests in itself because the world is full of men and women who like to fuck, so why not get paid to be laid.

I also know about companionship. Sometimes a person needs someone around for communication. I get that. I am not in a relationship with anyone. I have had intimate moments with people but nothing to the point I want him in the house. Mr. Peabody is the only one I trust. He has been with me for a long time.

To be honest, I think Mr. Peabody is the reason I haven't found anyone. I enjoy what we do. I enjoy our connection. Mr.

Peabody joined my company about 5 years ago around the age of 25. He was at that age that was rough around the edges and he just needed them to be smoothed out. So I did. We fucked for hours the first night he was hired.

He knew how to handle himself, mentally and physically. I loved his quiet thug type look. He looked like he could fuck you up real quick with a one-two punch. It would be over before it started. Yet he was just a gentle giant with a very serious glare.

I loved the way his dark chocolate skin glowed from the light of the fire as we fucked in front of the fireplace on the living room floor. I remember wrapping my legs around his waist as he rocked his hips along with mine. His body was tatted everywhere and I had a sick, twisted obsession with tattoos on a man that made me want to just - *lick them.*

After we finished, he asked if he had the job. We laughed because of the type of job it was. I told him that was an added perk to the position. He was just so easy to talk to like I had never had before. And for him to be so young, it was like how some black people say - *'he had been here before'* . He was wise beyond his years and he handled himself well. I would still have my occasional clients whom he was extremely aware of and yet he carried himself well.

I offered him to choose one of the girls if he wanted. He does, but only when the girl makes the advances first. He never chooses anyone but me and that is his own decision. Usually after his hook up with one of the girls, he comes back to me, showered and ready to fuck. I'm always waiting because I know us.

Brian is his first name. Mr. Brian Peabody. He is special to me. I didn't expect him to be so on point as he is, most guys aren't. But he is some kind of breed of man that just - *gets it*.

As I arrive at the office, Mr. Peabody has all of the ladies ready for me to meet. I walk into my office and look out across Lake Michigan and Millenium Park.

"Ms. McBride,"

"Yes?" I turn around and take a seat. "I'm ready, send in the first one," I stated. Mr. Peabody nodded and we began the process.

Each meeting took at least one and a half hours for each one with me completing the process and providing them with their accommodations and classes that will need to be attended. I wanted Penelope Matthews to be the last one as I had needed to gather additional information from her. Mr. Peabody returned as the last candidate exited.

"She's ready," he said standing at the door.

"How is she?" I wondered if I could get just a hint of her personality.

"She's fine. She's been communicating with all of the other girls while they were waiting to be called in the meeting room,"

"Interesting," I said looking at her file.

"She got a bit worried when she realized that the girls weren't coming back to the room," he went on to say.

"Oh, why?"

"She thought they were let go. I informed them they weren't, they were just gone for the day as the onboard process was completed and were no longer needed," he stated. I knew I could always count on him.

"Good, good. Thank you," I said as I adjusted in my chair and nodded. "You can send her in,"

Mr. Peabody nodded and walked over to the door. He exited and shortly after and in walks this cute and adorable young woman with red hair and freckles.

"Hello Ms. Penelope Matthews," I said standing, motioning her to take a seat in one of the chairs in front of my desk.

She stops and hesitates a bit. She looked around taking in the view and then her eyes landed on me.

"Wow," she blurted out nervously. "I'm sorry,"

"Penelope?" I call her name. She straightened up and focused. "Please come sit," I motioned again to the chairs. She slowly walks over to the chair in front and sits carefully. I smile and take a seat to begin the process.

"Penelope Ann Matthews," I stated her full name.

"Oh, you can call me Poppie," she smiled nervously and adjusted her outfit.

"Thank you, but to be professional I and everyone else will address you as Penelope," I said and her smile faded to a business-like smile. "During business hours, of course," I smiled at her and her face brightened.

She was as beautiful as I thought she would be.

I've found her.

Chapter 9 - Onboarding

Poppie

I couldn't believe what was happening to me. It had to be a dream. Shayla hooked me the fuck up for real. I couldn't believe I had stepped in the office of the Notorious Madame - Ms. Vanessa McBride. Her shit was tight. Everyone looked so nice in the office, just working a normal job. I must admit, it wasn't what I expected even though I really didn't have any idea what to expect, but it was definitely not this.

The office looked like any other office I had worked for my temp assignments. It had a huge sign above the front desk that read 'Elegant Industries'. I felt a bit out of place because I really didn't know what to expect. Shayla just told me to come to the office and let them know that I was Candidate #6.

I walked over to the desk wearing an outfit that Shayla bought for me. I know I looked presentable as she picked it out for me. Her style has improved dramatically and the idea that she can afford these things is something we've always dreamed about. I'm about to look nice up in here for real. She gave me a nice orange, wide leg pants with a crisp, white patterned blouse with orange and red blocks and puffy sleeves, matched with a small red purse which I wore across my body. Shayla and I wore the same size shoes so I just borrowed a pair of sky high peep toe platform ankle strap pumps with the red bottoms to complete my look.

"Hello," I said as I approached the desk. The woman behind the desk held up her finger as she was on a phone call, speaking to a person on a headset.

"Yes Sir, I will make sure she gets the message," she said as he typed on her keyboard. She looked like she enjoyed working here. "I'm sorry. How can I help you?"

"Uh, I was told to come here and tell you that I am Candidate #6," I said, sounding totally out of place. My heart started beating a bit faster with anticipation.

"Oh great," she said, smiling from ear to ear. " Hold on, I'll take you up. I just need to call a replacement," she said, picking up a walkie-talkie calling over to handle the desk.

"Hey, can I ask you a question?" I asked, looking around and just taking everything in.

"Yes sure," she said confidently.

"How is it working here, like for real?"

"It's amazing. The hotel industry is profitable therefore Ms. McBride is at the top of her game," she responded. Hotel industry? What the fuck did she just say?

"Excuse me, am I in the right place?" I said, sounding confused. She giggled as she had had that reaction before.

"Yes, you are. Ms. McBride owns the Elegant Hotels in and around Chicago. She also is the owner of Elegant Escorts. Actually, she has her hands in a lot of different businesses under the Elegant label," she confirmed.

"Oh, wow. I didn't know that. Damn,"

"I know it's a lot to take in, but it's amazing to work for her. She is an amazing woman. She's very encouraging and supportive of women," she went on to say. Finally, another petite woman walked up to the desk. "Great, I can take you up now, follow me."

She grabbed her tablet and phone and walked from behind the desk as the other woman replaced her. I followed her over to the elevators as I looked around and saw everyone doing some of everything. We rode up the elevator to the top floor and the view of Chicago was astonishing. I had never seen the city from this view. It was breathtaking.

I stopped at the window and looked out taking in everything.

"Isn't the view remarkable?" she said, waiting for me.

"Hey, question," I said, walking quickly to catch up with her. "What am I going to expect? What am I to do?"

"Just be yourself. She's nice," she smiled and led me to a conference room with 5 other ladies.

I walked in and took the last open seat.

"Thank you for coming ladies. In front of you, you will find a folder with your documents you will need to sign. Before we have you do that, Mr. Peabody will come and discuss all of the documents before you sign. If you have any questions, please direct them to him as he will be the best person to ask,"

"Well I have one question, who is Mr. Peabody?" The girl at the end of the table asked loudly. Everybody turned to the girl from the desk to answer the question. Just as she opened her mouth, the door quickly opened.

"I am Mr. Peabody," A gorgeous and delicious black man walked in the door, dressed in a dark blue suit and suede shoes. His scent permeated the room upon his entrance. His features were that of a thug motherfucker but he looked very intelligent. He was dressed to impress and this motherfucker did just that - he impressed me.

"Hello Mr. Peabody, I'll let you take it from here," she said and turned to exit the room.

"Thank you Stephanie," he said, closing the door behind her. He turned and walked to the front of the room.

"Hello everyone, I am Mr. Peabody. I am the assistant to Ms. McBride. Welcome to Elegant Escorts, which is under the umbrella of Elegant Industries, the company that owns and operates the Elegant Hotels," he stated, looking like a damn piece of chocolate.

He was Ms. McBride's assistant. He looked good as fuck. I watched him as he went on to explain the documents in our folders and what we were agreeing to upon signature. He was very professional and calm. He had the build of a running back on a football team and he was clean shaven. Shayla told me about him. He is the right hand man for Ms. McBride and he was fine as fuck. Shayla didn't go into too much detail about him, she just said that he is quiet but he will take care of everything that is needed.

After he explained all of the documents, he left for a bit as we signed our names to change our lives. I looked around the table and it was a group of women from all different backgrounds and ethnicities. I liked that in a company, they needed to hire everybody.

"So which one of y'all think Mr. Peabody looks good as fuck," A woman at the end of the table stated out loud. We all giggled and raised our hands.

"Girl, he is fine as fuck," another one said across the table.

"That's her assistant? I know she fucking that," another said.

"You think?" The third woman asked.

"I know I would," I chimed in. Everyone laughed. I liked this bunch of girls, we were all thinking the same thing.

"So where is everyone from?" The woman at the end of the table started. "I'm from Dolton. Not originally, but yeah," she said.

"I'm from the southside, Wild Hunnids," I replied.

"No shit? Damn, okay," she said.

"West side over here," The woman sitting next to me stated.

"I'm from Humboldt Park," The woman who sat across from me stated.

"So we are all pretty much from Chicago," The Dolton chick stated.

"Looks like it," I replied.

"Well, I'm Leddy y'all, nice to meet all of y'all," she said. Leddy was from Humboldt Park.

"Nice to meet you Leddy, I'm Poppie," I waved.

"Poppie? That's a cute name," Dolton girl said. "I'm Becky," she waved. I smiled and waved back.

"Hi,"

"Hello everyone, I'm Brianna and I'm from Naperville. I ran into Ms. McBride at a just the right time in my life, because I really needed a job,"

"I feel you Brianna," Becky replied. "She found me outside the police station. I had just made bail when she asked me what I wanted to do with my life,"

"Yeah, she did the same with me. I thought she was crazy at first, but she didn't pressure me and told me to call her when I was ready to 'change my life,'" another woman chimed in. "I'm Ari, I'm from New York,"

"Damn, New York?" Becky blurted while we all looked at her.

"Yup, she found me on the streets. Told me to get clean and come work for her. She put me up in a hotel while I was detoxing," she said lowering her head.

"Damn, you sound like me. My friend told me about her. She helped my friend when she got out of jail. My friend found me at just the right time and told me to come see Ms. McBride. My friend got me clean and here I am," I had told my story. The other girls around the table were all shaking their heads in agreement.

We all had a story that led us to Ms. McBride. That made me even more intrigued about who she is and why did she start this company? I know this Bitch had a lot of fucking money. I wondered how she had so much money to do all of this. What was she getting out of it?

Mr. Peabody returned into the room and went over the paperwork to ensure we had signed them all correctly. He was soft spoken and he was nice. He smiled every once in a while, talking to each person individually. When he spoke with us, he was very attentive and alert. He made us feel what we had to say was important and he was really interested. He made everyone feel calm and relaxed.

After all of the paperwork was completed the process began in which we would all individually meet Ms. McBride. I was nervous as fuck. I didn't want to go first, I felt as if I had to pee instantly.

"I will call your name and you are to gather all of your things and follow me," Mr. Peabody said as he looked at his tablet. "Ms. Leddy Gonzales," he called. All eyes went to Leddy.

She looked nervous but pretty. She had long, black hair flowing down her back with a hairpin on one side of her hair. She grabbed her purse, water bottle and keys and followed Mr. Peabody out of the room. Everything got quiet amongst us as we didn't know what to expect. I figured I would ask her when she returned what to expect. I think everyone would want to know honestly.

As the time ticked down, an hour and a half had passed and she hadn't returned. Mr. Peabody entered with his tablet and called the next person, "Ms. Becky Stanford," he quietly said.

Becky looked around as she grabbed her messenger bag and walked out the room. It was then I realized Leddy didn't return. I started to overthink the situation to the point I was wondering if something went wrong.

When he returned again and neither Becky or Leddy returned with him, I started to worry.

"Um, Mr. Peabody," I said, raising my hand slightly.

"Yes, Ms. Matthews?" he said. He knew exactly who I was. It threw me off a bit as I didn't expect him to know me right away.

"Um, is everything okay?" I asked. He looked confused a bit. He walked over to me directly.

"What do you mean?"

"I just noticed that the others didn't come back,"

"Oh," he said. He smiled a soft smile at me for reassurance. "Understood. No worries. They were allowed to leave as they have completed the on-boarding process and are no longer needed for the remainder of the day," he said confidently.

"Oh, I'm sorry, I was just.."

"It's okay, everything is fine. You were referred to by Shayla, correct?" he asked, looking at me directly in my eyes. His eye contact was a bit intense.

"Uh, yes," I said looking down, breaking contact. He tipped my chin up to make eye contact again.

"First rule, keep eye contact. It will be beneficial working here. I know it can be uncomfortable at times but keep your cool and you will learn how to control it to the point it won't be," he said. I nodded my head and kept eye contact. This brotha was well put together.

"Ok, thank you,"

"Don't worry, everything will be fine. Shayla is my girl. She told me about you," he said softly.

"She did?" I said surprisingly. Shayla was my girl as she always had my back.

"Yeah, she did. I'm glad you came. Ms. McBride will take good care of you. She's excited to meet you," he said smiling. He put me at ease. I see why Ms. McBride had him as an assistant. He knew exactly how to make us feel.

"Thanks, I am too," I smiled in return and he called the next candidate. She followed him in and I patiently waited for my name to be heard.

I was there all day and the last one to be called into the office. I walked slowly behind Mr. Peabody as he opened the door to Ms. McBride's office. The decor was white and black everywhere. Her desk was a huge black desk at the far end of the office with the city view behind her. I walked in and looked around as I could see Lake Michigan and the park down below.

"Penelope?" Ms. McBride called my name. I had lost focus at the view. She was beautiful standing at her desk. Her brown skin looked like satin as her long silky, brown hair cascaded on her shoulders. "Please come sit," she said pointing at the chairs in front of her desk.

I slowly walked over and carefully took a seat in front of her. She smiled and sat down. Ms. McBride was well put together and not a hair out of place. She wore her clothes well and she looked like money.

"Penelope Ann Matthews," she stated my government name.

"Oh, you can call me Poppie," I said. It slipped out before I could contain it. I was so used to saying it.

"Thank you, but to be professional I and everyone else will address you as Penelope," she said directly. My smile faded nervously. "During business hours, of course," she smiled and winked at me.

My spirits lifted with her reassuring gesture. She was just breaking the ice. I liked that.

"Oh great," I said smiling.

"Mr. Peabody tells me that you were referred to by Shayla, is that correct?" she said looking up from my file.

"Uh, yes ma'am. She told me all about the position,"

"Good, I like Shayla. She's grown a lot. I see a lot of myself in her. I can't wait to see what she does. And with you as well," she said smiling at me.

"What do you mean?" I was a bit confused on what she was really saying.

"Penelope," she said, sitting back and crossing her legs and arms. "I want the ladies to be the best at what they do and be encouraged to find something that drives them and make it happen. I want to grow business women who know their worth and give them the opportunity to make something of themselves when society has given up on them," she said. It was like she was a savior for all of the girls who have been dealt a bad hand.

"Wow," I couldn't believe I was in her presence. She was phenomenal.

"I expect nothing less from you either," she said, returning back to my folder.

"Yes ma'am,"

"Good. You will start classes on Monday. I hear you would like to learn Mandarin,"

"Yes, I've always wanted to learn a language and I like the sound of the Chinese language,"

"Understood. Mandarin is a great language to know. We have several clients who speak Mandarin and they feel comfortable with those who can communicate with them. Sometimes the meaning can get lost in the translation, therefore they are grateful when one of our ladies can speak their language,"

"Awesome," I responded.

"Great. You will also attend etiquette courses and fine dining as well. Do you know how to cook?" she asked as she wrote notes in file.

"No, unfortunately not,"

"No worries, Mr. Peabody teaches a cooking class once a week, I'll sign you up for it, " she said as she continued to write. She opened her desk drawer and pulled out a small case.

She placed the case on the desk and opened it. Inside she had what looked like a hotel room key. She looked at the number and placed it on the paperwork in front of her.

"Here is your key for your accommodations. You can bring your items there so you will feel more comfortable while in the beginning stages,"

"Beginning stages?" I asked.

"Yes, you have a lot to learn therefore you are at the beginning. It usually takes about 3-4 months to get where I need you to be before you are scheduled for appointments," she responded.

"Oh,"

"If you need assistance bringing your belongings, tell Mr. Peabody he will help you," she said as she opened another drawer and pulled out a cell phone. "Here is your work phone. Please have it with you at all times, especially when you have been assigned to a client," she said, passing it over to me. I'm sure she already has the number written down.

"Thank you," I said, checking out the phone. It was an android phone but a good one. I'm sure she is trying to make sure all her ducks are in a row.

"The phones have a tracking app on it should you need any assistance," she said smiling and closing my folder. "I'm glad you joined us Penelope, I'm sure you will do well here," she said smiling.

"Thank you for having me," I said in return. Shit, this woman has just given me a place to stay rent free and a cell phone. She had already done more than what I expected.

"FYI, these rooms are on a floor in one of my hotels, however they are designed like apartments, so you won't have to worry any guests of the hotels on that level as they do not have access," she mentioned.

"Oh wow," I said looking at the key. I didn't know what else to say.

"Do you have any questions, Penelope?"

"No ma'am, you've pretty much covered everything that I can think of," I replied.

"Well good, but if you think of anything, Mr. Peabody's number is listed in the phone along with mine as well," she said standing up and coming around the desk.

I stood up and faced her. She held out her hand to shake my hand. I took hold of it and she had a grip like a man, it was tight and direct as she squeezed my hand as she shook it.

"Welcome aboard Penelope. I expect great things from you," she said, softly patting the back of my hand.

"I won't let you down, Ms. McBride, promise," I said, holding her hand as well.

"I know you won't Penelope. I have a good feeling about you."

Chapter 10 - Celebration

Poppie

I turned the key and walked into my very own apartment, for a temporary basis but I don't mind at all. The view was that of another building but I didn't give a fuck, I had views! I could see other taller and shorter buildings and if I stand in the corner of the living room and press my face against the glass, I could catch a glimpse of the lake.

The apartment was fully furnished with everything I needed as I didn't have much to bring over as Ms. McBride suggested I do. I opened the refrigerator and it was fully stocked with drinks, fruits and vegetables. It also had a selection of meats, cheeses and frozen foods in the bottom freezer. On the counter was a gift card with $200 for Walmart with a note: *"Please purchase any extra items you may need."*

"Shit," I said out loud. I couldn't believe it. I had come up for real. Now all I need to do is stay there.

I walked into my bedroom and it was as large as my old apartment. I opened the walk-in closet and all of my clothes were hanging there. They hardly took up space in the closet. I could finally go on a shopping spree. I'll do that after my first check. I wanted to get started with my classes first and learn as much as I can.

I wanted to catch up to Shayla.

Suddenly, there was a knock at my door. I didn't know who knew I was here so I was curious to see who it was.

I peeped through the peephole, it was Shayla. Right on time.

"Shayla!" I screamed as I opened the door. She smiled so hard and grabbed me and we hugged and jumped around.

"Awww shit, look at you Poppie," she said as we let go of each other and walked inside the apartment to get out of the hallway.

"I know right! Look at this shit! Oh my goodness Shayla!"

"I told you," Shayla said as she walked around checking out the apartment.

"I mean, I don't know how to thank you," I said, almost breaking down in tears.

"Naw, Bitch, don't start," she said, raising her finger at me. "You gonna make me start," she said wiping under her eyes.

"It's just, nobody....ever...,"

"I know girl. You know I know,"

We sat down on the couch in the living room and sat in silence for a minute just taking all of it in.

"I remember when I was in the beginning stages. Shit, it wasn't too long ago," she said as she opened her purse and pulled out a package containing two blunts.

"That's what I'm talking about," I said, scooting over next to her and picking up an ashtray from the side table.

"Oh that's another thing, we have a hook up on the weed as well," she said as he lit the perfectly rolled blunt. The aroma filled the air with a scent I missed.

"For real?"

"Call Mr. Peabody, he'll hook you up," she said as she passed the blunt to me.

"Question," I said, inhaling the smoke and blowing out circles, it had been a while. "Wassup with Mr. Peabody?"

"What you mean?"

"You know, does he hook up with anyone?" I asked, curious if he was available.

"Well, the word is he caters to Ms. McBride, however he has been known to hook up with a few girls every now and then. I haven't tried though, that's just too close for comfort for me,"

"I feel you. Interestingly, Ms. McBride got her 'boo thang' running shit. Wait, does she still have clients?"

"Yes. She has very high profile clients. She does what she does, so well,"

"Man, to be that woman, it must be fantastic," I said, inhaling again and passing it back to Shayla.

"I'm sure it is. She has a lot of money to play and do as she wishes,"

"True," I sat back and kicked my shoes off and looked around. This was all me. I planned to jump right into my classes so I can get better and better.

"So Monday is your first day of classes,"

"Yeah, what should I expect?"

"School. That's basically it. You go to the same place you came from today but on a lower floor. It's set up just like classrooms and you learn everything you need to do what I do," she said, taking a puff.

"Damn, she got it all hooked up huh?"

"Yup she does."

"Do you still attend classes?" I wondered if she was finished with all of this learning stuff. I didn't mind it, I'm just not the best at it.

"Yes, you never stop learning. It's amazing. I'm learning about business right now trying to figure out about owning my business,"

"Really, that would be nice. What would you want to do?"

"I'm not sure yet, but I have time to find out my options,"

"True. Have you talked to Mike?" she looked at me and I instantly knew that she hadn't.

"Naw," she said, she didn't want to answer. "He ain't getting out for a long time and I can't mess up my good thing I got going on."

"I feel you, do what you gotta do,"

"Hey, you wanna go shopping?" she asked, putting out the blunt in the ashtray.

"You buying?" I asked because I have no money.

"Yes,"

"Then yes ma'am!" I yelled. Shayla laughed as I put my shoes back on, grabbed my bag and was out the door. I was gonna love this new lifestyle of mine.

Vanessa

"Ms. McBride," Mr. Peabody called as he entered my office. I had finally found her. I was happy my search was finally over.

"Yes Mr. Peabody," I turned around in my chair to face him. I was beaming.

"We have completed the on-boarding for today," he said, waiting for my next request.

"Today was a good day, Mr. Peabody. I think we should celebrate," I said smiling. I reached down to put my shoes back on as I had removed them shortly after Penelope left.

Mr. Peabody saw me reaching for my shoes and walked over to assist me. He took my foot gently in his hand as he slipped my shoe on my right foot. His touches made my skin burn as he held my ankle while fastening the strap.

"How would you like to celebrate tonight?" he asked while reaching for my other foot.

"Hmmm, let me think," I said. He glanced up at me and snickered. He continued to fasten the strap on my other shoe. "Have you taken care of the Governor and his request for his grandson?"

He stood up and folded his arms behind him, "Yes, all of the details have been completed and the associates have been selected waiting for your final approval, which is on your desk right here," he said pointing at a file folder that sat at least 2 inches high on my desk.

That was the Governor's file. Anything and everything having to do with him gets added to his file, regardless if it's for him or his grandson and his college buddies.

"Good, I knew you would be on top of things," I stood up and faced him just inches away.

"Not quite,"

"What do you mean? What else are you not on top of?"

"You," he said confidently. This motherfucker was smooth as hell. I smiled and kissed his lips as he pulled me closer to him.

I could feel his manhood grow against my stomach. I sucked his tongue into my mouth, tasting its sweetness as it filled my mouth completely.

"Well we will have to do something about that, now won't we?" I said softly as I pulled away.

"Yes Ma'am," he said, clearing his throat.

Mr. Peabody had the driver come to pick us up to drive us home. Mr. Peabody lives at the mansion along with me as I like to have him available to me at all times. As we pulled into the driveway, I was happy to be home and happy that I had ended my search.

My son, Sam, exited the house as Mr. Peabody and I walked towards the door.

"Hello Mother," he said as he kissed me on my cheek. "Mr. Peabody," he said, holding out his hand to greet him. Mr. Peabody shook his hand followed by a 'bro hug'.

"Where are you headed off to?" I asked, curious. I wondered if he had found someone special.

"I'm going to hang out with a few friends. I won't be out too late," he said smiling.

"Any young ladies, I know about?" I said, raising my voice as he walked away.

"Good night, Mother," he said, waving off as he walked to the garage.

"That boy, will he ever find someone?"

"Some may say the same about you," Mr. Peabody quipped with a grin. I turned and looked at him slyly.

"I already have," I said walking past him and inside the house. Mr. Peabody smiled as he shook his head.

I stepped inside and removed my shoes. It was nice being at home. Now to have some 'me' time.

"Mr. Peabody," I said, grabbing my shoes and turning around before heading to my bedroom.

"Yes Ma'am," he said, stopping and giving me his full attention.

"Meet me in my bedroom in 1 hour," I said, placing a kiss on his lips and turned away. I heard him clear his throat.

"As you wish."

After an hour passed, I waited for Mr. Peabody to return. I heard a soft knock at my door and I smiled. He was always on time.

"Enter," I said and the door opened. Mr. Peabody walked in with a tray of goodies; a bottle of wine, strawberries, grapes and pineapple circles. He knows me so well. I don't know if I am holding him back from his full potential or if he is happy to be where he is. He doesn't complain and I am not holding him hostage as he is free to leave at any given moment.

Mr. Peabody placed the tray down on the cocktail table in the sitting area of my room. He wore a thick, gray microfiber robe, tied around his waist and wore suede house shoes on his feet. I knew he was totally naked underneath as I wore the same exact thing.

"You are so prompt,"

"I enjoy every moment I have with you," he said walking over to me. He leaned down and planted a sweet kiss upon my lips.

"Shall we?" I said.

"Yes," he said, turning to pick up the tray. He followed me into my master bathroom which basically was almost the size of my bedroom.

He placed the tray on a side table alongside the bathtub. He started the water in the tub and poured in lavender oil along with rose petals. He went around the bathroom lighting candles and an aroma candle.

The water began to steam as I stood next to the bath. He walked over to me, his eyes never leaving mine, and pulled my belt untying my robe. The robe opened revealing my voluptuous breasts and my body in all its glory. I pulled the belt on his robe and opened to reveal his naked body, his chocolate skin reflecting the light from the candles as they danced around the room.

He pulled me closer as I took hold of his shaft. He was erect and ready. I stroked him slowly as he leaned down and kissed my neck, biting and giving me chills with every touch. His breathing altered as I continued to stroke him slowly between my fingers.

"Are you ready to get in?" he asked, stepping back and gaining control.

"Yes," I said as he held out his hand and helped me into the huge bathtub built for two.

The hot water stung my skin as I stepped into the water and lowered myself until the water covered my waist. Mr. Peabody stepped in, opposite of me, his dick swinging above the water as he stepped carefully so as to not step on me. He slowly lowered himself with his legs resting on either side of me.

"Brian," I called his name. This was our time, away from the office and everyone else. "Are you happy?"

"Yes I am, Vanessa. Why do you always ask?" I love when he calls my name. His voice sounds so sexy when my name crosses his lips.

He picks up a strawberry and holds it for me to take a bite. I love the way he watches me as I take a bite. He smiles and eats the remainder.

"I just want to make sure you are," I said, raising my foot out of the water, holding it over him as I watched the water drip on his chest. He took hold of my foot in his hands as he smoothed the water over my skin.

"I am. Always," he said leaning forward as he kissed my toes. He watched me as he slipped his tongue between my toes. I squirmed as he knew exactly how to get me started.

He sucked each toe individually in his mouth and tickled them with his tongue. It made my love spot quiver with anticipation as I wanted to feel him deep inside me. Brian ran his hands down my leg as he placed my foot on his shoulder while he scooted closer.

I laid my head back against the tube enjoying his touches as he took my other foot and gave the same attention to my other toes. I closed my eyes and enjoyed feeling his lips wrap my toes. He massaged my calves, squeezing them with just enough pressure to give me the pain I desired.

I opened my eyes and looked at him as he released my legs. He sat waiting for my orders as he put his arms on the sides of the tub. I carefully stood up before him as the water trickled off my hard nipples and down my body. He licked his lips as he glanced over my body. He enjoyed fucking me and I enjoyed fucking him too.

I waded over to him and he closed his legs as I stepped over him. My pussy faced him directly. He slid his wet hands up my thighs and grabbed my hips as he leaned forward to give my *garden* a kiss. He buried his face in my vajayjay as I held his head for stability. He raised my right foot and placed it on the side of the tub, allowing him better access.

I felt his widened tongue slowly lick my tulips fully and completely. He held onto my thighs as I held his head in place while he ate my sweetness. My eyes closed and my head fell back as I enjoyed feeling his suck my clit. The warmth of his tongue moving over my fleshy folds sent a slow chill across my body giving me rolling goosebumps along my skin.

"Mmmmm Brian," I moaned softly. "That feels so good," He grabbed my ass and pulled me closer as he devoured my pussy. His eyes closed as he drank my flowing juices from deep within.

"Mmmmm," he moaned as he sucked my clit. I began to shake as he sucked it hard, bringing me pain and pleasure.

He planted small kisses along my snatch as he lowered my leg back into the water. As I stood before Brian, he picked up my saturated loofah and added my favorite body wash.

I turned around as he began washing my legs, ass, and back.

"Brian, do you think Sam would get upset if I found someone for him?"

"I think it depends," he said as he rubbed circles along my back.

"How so?" I said turning around. He continued scrubbing my body with the loofah as he made circles across my breasts.

"Well, does he know you are looking for someone for him?"

"He knows I want him with someone, like any mother would want for her son,"

"True,"

"And he is aware that I'm looking. He has agreed to go on a few dates in the past,"

"Also true," he said as he dipped the loofah in the water. "But has he connected with any of the ladies you set up for him?" he said as I sat down in the water.

The soap suds melted off as I lowered my body further in the water. The water was now full of bubbles floating on top of the water, leaving it hard to see below the surface.

"He has not, which is the reason why I think I have found the one," I said as he stood up before me.

His body glistened as the water slithered down his dark chocolate frame. His satin skin looked tantalizing in the candlelight, his tattoos beckoning me. I loved his chiseled body with tattoos patterned across his body. The sight of his wet body reminded me of the naked D'Angelo video in which his body was sexy as hell, all brown, toned in just the right places and looking very snackable. I know for a fact a lot of women were wet after watching that video. Yet here I was getting a version right in front of me.

His dick hung to the side, thick and semi-erect as he began to wash himself. I watched as he cleaned himself for me. I watched the suds slowly slicing down his arms, chest and abs.

"Do you really think she is the one?"

"My gut tells me yes, but we shall see in the next few months," I said as I watched him squeezing the excess water over his face and down his chest.

I took hold of his member and began to stroke it awake. He watched me as I stroked him in a twisting motion. I raised myself to my knees and licked him from his scrotum up his shaft taking him inside my mouth.

He inhaled as his head fell back. His breathing altered as I sucked him slowly in and out while playing with his balls.

"Vanessa," he moaned softly. "Yesssssss....mmmmhmmm,"

I sucked his head slowly past my lips and into my mouth. He placed his arms behind his back as he usually does while I sucked his cock in and out my mouth.

"Uuuhhh, Uhhhh... Mmmm..Vanessa," he moaned again as he leaned back while I stroked him. I slowly released him and stood up. He kissed me deeply, groping my wet ass. I stepped out of the tub as did he, grabbing the tray from the side of the tub with the fruit.

I walked back to my bedroom and laid across one side of the bed as he followed, placing the tray on the other side of the bed. Brian came to my side of the bed as I reached for a pineapple slice and placed it on the head of his dick.

"Funny," he said, looking down at me.

"Yummy," I replied as I started sucking and eating the pineapple.

"Ahh, Vanessa, what are you doing to me?"

"Tasting you," I said as I licked and took another bit of the fruit. "Licking you," I popped his tip in my mouth as I licked around the sides. "Pleasing you,"

"My turn," he said, pulling himself from my mouth and pushing me back whilst raising my legs. I swallowed the pineapple and watched as he took control.

He spread my legs wide as he plunged his face into my love nest. He held my legs open as he sucked my juices that flowed out my cavern. Brian slowly licked my clit and hummed along my lips.

"Uhhh....uuuuhhhh....Uuummmm...uuuuhhh...Brian,"   I moaned as I squeezed my tits. My nipples hardened as he ate his meal.

"You taste so good," he whispered from between my legs. He continued to munch as I quivered with every taste.

"Brian," I moaned. "Uhhhh....uhhhh...,"

"Yes Vanessa,"

"I want to feel you," I said as I caressed his head between my legs. He quickly stopped and planted kisses all over my body as he made his way up to my lips.

"As you wish," he said as he stood over me. He plunged his cock deep inside my honey pot as he laid upon me.

"Uuuhhh," I cried. I closed my eyes and enjoyed him sliding his thick shaft inside me, filling me completely and hitting my spot.

"Mmmm you feel so good," he groaned as he began grinding is dick further inside, touching my special spot with each entry.

"Mmm, Uhh.. uhhh..yes.. Uuhhh," I wailed as we rocked together simultaneously.

"Uuuhhh....Uhhhh...Uhhh....Vanessa...Mmmhhh baby," he muttered as he increased his speed.

He looked at me, his mouth open as he pumped deep inside me. Brian leaned down and kissed me hard as he quickened his pace.

"Fuck...it...baby....fuck....it...fuck....it...baby...yesssss," I said as he thrusted his cock deep inside, forcing me to release my nectar all over his meaty shaft.

"Uhhh ... .uhhh...Uhhh...shit....ooooo....fuck.," he said as my juices covered him allowing him to slide in and out easily, my juiciness sloshing around and oozing down my ass.

"Don't cum yet," I demanded as he held onto my hips; he was now banging my pussy as I held my legs spread eagle. My toes curled with each thrust.

"Vanessa, I....uhh...I...uuhh.....I..," he begged.

"No, not yet, uuhhh.....not....yet...," I begged him. I wanted him to reach his climax with me. I was almost there as I watched him plunge himself between my legs.

"Uhhh...uhhh...I...I...fuck....,"

"Ooooooo...shit.....I.....I...," I moaned. I could feel his dick harden as he banged forcefully inside.

"Uhhhh...Uhhhh...Uhhhh..uhhhh.....mmmhhh   ...
.mmmmm," he wailed as the bed was now making noises. He fucked me hard as he was about to release himself deep inside.

"Cum   for   me   baby....cum   for meeeee......aaaaaaaaaaaahhhh," I screamed as I reached my climax while he fucked my spot hard.

He groaned and groaned as he watched my cream cover all over his thick shaft.

"Uuuuuuuuhhhhhhhhhhh......aaaaaaaaahhhhhhhhhh,"   he growled as I felt his hot jism release deep inside my cavern. He pounded hard and quick strokes as he released his army. Brian collapsed on top of me, still grinding his hips to release every drop.

I kissed him softly as he shivered while coming down from ecstasy. I sucked on his tongue and I planted sweet kisses on his lips.

He ended with small kisses while he slowly released himself from me. He walked to the bathroom returning with a washcloth and dry towel for clean up.

After we tidied up, we laid next to each other cuddling in our robes eating fruit as I laid across him, my head laying on his lap. I opened my mouth as he popped in a delicious grape.

"You're dangerous Vanessa," he said as he smoothed back a few loose strands of hair from my hair bun.

"I know, but you love it,"

"I do," he responded.

"How much?" I asked, already knowing the answer. I turned to face him and he caressed my face.

"More than you know."

Chapter 11 - Peabody

Poppie

Classes started just like Shayla said. I had etiquette, language and yoga classes in the morning and culinary, finances and self defense classes in the evening. Every night my ass was tired. Shayla wasn't lying when she said they would have me doing a bit of everything all at once. It was cool though because I had nothing else to do.

Shayla was finished on my level therefore she was in none of my classes. So I had to make some friends. I had classes with a few of the girls that were onboarding with me. Leddy from Humboldt Park was in my etiquette class and Becky from Dolton was in my self defense class.

"Hey Poppie," Leddy said as I entered the class and sat down at the desk next to her.

"Hey Leddy girl,"

"Girl, did you hear that Becky tried to get with Mr. Peabody?" she asked, looking at me to see if I knew.

"What? Are you serious?" Of course, I didn't know. "Wait, how? Why? What the fuck?"

"I know right?"

"What was she thinking?"

"Well word around here is that he will get down and dirty with some of the girls every once in a while. But he's real picky,"

"Real picky? That makes no sense. I heard he and Ms. McBride got a 'thing' going on and shit," I responded.

Leddy's eyes grew instantly.

"Did you find out what happened?"

"Yeah, he told her that he wasn't able to accommodate her just yet, but he will keep her in mind later," she said.

"What the fuck does that mean?" I asked.

"I don't know," she straightened up as the instructor walked in and closed the door.

"Shit, well I'll find out when I see her in my last class," I said as the instructor came to the front.

Becky wanted to try out Mr. Peabody. Shit, I don't blame her. That motherfucker looks good and looks like he can fuck better. I just know he laid that pipe good as hell. I see why Ms. McBride is walking tall with no complaints. She gets her back blown out on a daily basis. I can't help but be impressed.

Shayla and I had lunch together since we were in the same building. It was nice to be able to work with her. Shit, it was nice to be able to work for Ms. McBride. She was a woman who I look up to as she has her shit on point. She thought about everything that would be needed for her company to flourish.

I was shocked as shit when Shayla took me to the cafeteria. It was a full service cafeteria that served breakfast, lunch and dinner. The cafeteria stayed open until 9 pm for those who take the evening classes, therefore dinner was served for them as well.

"She owns the entire building," Shayla said as we sat down to devour lunch.

"Really, well damn. She has god-like money,"

"Pretty much," Shayla answered.

"Hey about Mr. Peabody," I started and Shayla squinted her eyes at me.

"What?"

"Girl, I hope you not thinking about hittin' and quittin' with him,"

"I'm not. I'm curious, but not interested. But that motherfucker is fine,"

"That he is,"

"Okay, so he does get down with some of the girls?"

"He does. I've seen him take a few of them out. But it's like simple fuck and then he's back to Vanessa's side. She got him on a long leash and she knows how hard to pull it,"

"Damn,"

"Why do you ask?"

"Oh, one to the girls I joined with she apparently tried to get up with him,"

"Did she really?" she chuckled. "He turned her down right?"

"How did you know?" I asked, leaning in and learning more and more.

"He won't fuck around with a newbie. She needs to at least complete the first level of classes before he even thinks about it," she answered.

"How'd you know?"

"Because a girl who was onboarding with me, did the same thing," she answered.

"Oh wow,"

I'm sure Mr. Peabody got tired of the newbies hitting on him, but I couldn't blame them. Especially being in this type of business, who wouldn't try when a nice looking man is available at your beckon call.

"But eventually, he will get with an occasional girl every now and then. But like I said, its just a good fuck and then back to work,"

"Well shit, sometimes that's all a bitch needs," We both laughed at the truth. We finished up lunch and headed back to class for the remainder of the day.

While passing in the hallway over to my remaining classes, I noticed Mr. Peabody speaking to Ari from New York in the hallway. She didn't look too well and Mr. Peabody was speaking with the instructor. I hope she was okay. This shit looked so much like high school and Mr. Peabody was the Assistant Principal.

I finally got to my last class with Becky from Dolton. I couldn't wait to find out the juicy escapades directly from the horse's mouth.

"Hey Becky," I said as I walked over to the mat she was sitting on.

"Hey Poppie, wassup?"

"Girl you know I heard and I gotta know from you,"

"Yes I did," she smirked. "And he told me it wasn't a good time because I just started. He told me to finish my first level and then check back with him."

"Damn, for real?" I was shocked.

"Yup,"

"You know he belongs to Vanessa, right?"

"Yeah, I know. But I also heard that he dips out every once in a while. Besides, she got her own thing going on. Did you know she still has clients?"

"Yup high profile ones,"

"Yup, the bitch is bad." We both shook our heads in agreement.

"I wanna be like her," Both of us said in unison. We giggled because we were thinking alike.

"Well, let me know when you hit it, I'm curious," I said.

"You'll be the first to know." Becky said, winking at me.

She's had her eye on him since day one.

He fucks with Vanessa.

She ain't ready.

Months flew by and the next thing I knew, we had learned so much, shit was just coming naturally. I felt improved and I felt like I had learned to become a better version of myself.

I learned Mandarin, Spanish and I'm learning Italian. Vanessa was impressed as well, she sent me a token of appreciation for my hard work - it was a rust colored, *Hermes Tilt Bag!* It included a note: *Poppie, I saw this and instantly thought of you. It reminded me of your hair. Congratulations and Enjoy!*

I was in the moment, enjoying my gift when someone knocked on my door. I went to the door expecting it to be one of the girls on my floor or Shayla yet I stood corrected - It was Mr. Peabody.

"Mr. Peabody," I said, sounding surprised he would be at my door.

"Hello Ms. Matthews, I'm not disturbing you am I?" he asked, standing tall looking handsome in a nice navy blue suit. I get weak in the knees when I see a good looking man in a suit.

"Uh, no. Not at all, please come in," I said, holding the door open so he could enter.

He passed me as I closed the door behind him and I inhaled his cologne. This man ALWAYS smelled good. He stood by the couch and waited for me to join him in the living room.

"Please sit," I said, motioning him to sit down. "For what do I owe this visit?"

He smiled and took a seat after unbuttoning his suit jacket. He held a manila envelope that was about a half inch thick.

"Well, Poppie," he started. I smiled that he was comfortable calling me by my nickname. "I have been instructed to get you up-to-date on your first assignment," he said, handing me the envelope.

"Really? So soon?" I didn't think it would happen as quickly as it did but I was ready to show my shit.

"Yes, You have excelled well and Ms. McBride is very pleased. She's had her eye on you since day one," he said, sitting back and getting comfortable.

"Seriously? Why me?"

"She said you remind her of someone," he said, opening his jacket and pulling out a silver case. He opened and it was filled with fully rolled blunts! "Do you mind?"

"Hell naw!" I said sliding the ashtray over to him. He chuckled, pulled out a zippo light and lit the end of the blunt.

"Oh, I have something for you as well," he said, opening the other side of his jacket. He pulled out a velvet bag and handed it to me.

The instant I opened it, I could smell the fresh aroma of marijuana. I looked at him like he was Santa Claus. He smiled and nodded.

"Shayla told me you needed some," he said.

"I did, thank you," I said, closing the bag. "So how does this work?" I asked, tapping on the envelope.

"You will report to the office tomorrow, on the same floor you went to for onboarding. There you will be briefed on the gentleman you will be escorting. All the details will be discussed at that time," he said, going no further.

"Ok, cool," I said as he passed the blunt to me.

"So how are you doing? Getting along with everything?"

"Yeah, I guess. Shit this is the best I've ever had it,"

"Feels like a dream, huh?"

"Yeah, one that I don't want to wake from,"

"I feel you on that. I remembered when I joined Ms. McBride. She has a way of coming in your life at just the right time,"

"Ain't that the truth," I said, taking a long puff. Mr. Peabody stared and smiled at me for a while and then abruptly stood up.

"Well, I must leave," he said walking over to the door.

"What about this?" I said holding the blunt.

"Smoke it, I have plenty. Call if you need anything," he said as he opened the door.

"I will," I said as he walked out leaving me holding the door. As I slowly closed the door, I saw him stop at Becky from Dolton's door.

If she ain't ready, she better be, 'cause he has come knocking!

Mr. Peabody

As soon as I drove through the gates and into the garage, I saw Sam exiting his car.

"Hey Peabody," he said, coming over to me and shaking my hand.

"Wassup Bro, you just got in?"

"Yeah, I *just* got home from work. How about you?" he asked, stretching his arms above his head.

"Same," I said as I grabbed my bag from the backseat and closed the door.

"So Peabody," Sam said as he looked at me. "What is Mom up to?"

"What do you mean?"

"C'mon Bro," he said, looking skeptic. "You of all people know how my Mom is,"

I smiled and shook my head. "Yeah, I do."

"What is she up to?" he asked, looking for me to give him a straight answer.

"You already know your mother, I shouldn't have to tell you," I said, pulling out another blunt to smoke.

"That's the problem. She is trying to fix me up with all these women. I can find my own woman," he said as I passed the lit blunt to him. He inhaled deeply and blew out the smoke.

"True, but you know her. No woman will ever be good enough for you if you pick her. You know your mother, she wants the best for you,"

"Yeah, I know," he said, passing back the blunt. "So where are you coming from? And don't say work," he said looking at me slyly. He smiled and I smiled back shaking my head. I would never reveal where I've been because I don't speak about what I do outside of business hours.

"Trust me, it was work," I smiled, gave him a wink and left the garage to go find Vanessa.

I hurried up the stairs and down the corridor to my bedroom. I pulled off every stitch of clothing and immediately jumped into the shower.

My skin burned as I scrubbed myself clean under the hot water. I wanted to make sure no traces were left. I only wanted her to smell me, and no one else. I knew I would take another shower after, but I wouldn't rush to do so afterwards with her. I loved her scent on me.

After the shower, I grabbed my robe and headed over to her room. I heard music playing as I stepped closer to the door.

I knocked softly. The music lowered and she spoke, "You may enter."

That was my cue. I entered and closed and locked the door behind me. As I turned the corner to her bedroom, I saw her laying on the bed, dressed in nothing but the tossed bed sheets.

"I've been waiting for you," she said smiling. "Come here," she requested. I obliged.

"As you wish,"

Chapter 12 - Fraternity Boys

Poppie

I went to the briefing for my assignment and it was to accompany a few wealthy young men to a charity event. This was my first assignment and I was ready to do this shit. It was a lot easier to handle since it was a group of guys, we had to be in deep - we had a group of women. All of us were onboarding. I can only assume that there were more than one on-boarding class because some of the girls who were included, I had no idea who they were.

It was cool though because Becky from Dolton, Leddy from Humboldt Park and Ari from New York were there to join me. Since we all lived in the same building, the company arranged for us to have a driver available for us to arrive with the guys. I was given the grandson of the Governor.

Richard Anthony Fitzgerald III was the grandson of Governor Fitzgerald, who is one of Vanessa's clients. All of the guys were at his home therefore 7 cars arrived at his mansion to greet them.

"So ladies," I said as I exited the suv. "Y'all ready to have some fun,"

"It's about time, I've been waiting for this," Becky said.

"Me too," Leddy said as we walked side by side towards the entrance of this massive home.

"Same here," Ari chimed in as we reached the door.

It opened up to a huge foyer area and there stood young men in tuxedos. They looked damn good. Rich boys. I was about to enjoy this for real. They were enjoying themselves with a few refreshments before the party with a table filled with drinks and finger foods.

"Ladies!" One of them said as we entered. He approached us with his arms held wide as he held a glass of what I can only assume as champagne in one hand. "Welcome," The guys turned and walked to the middle of the room to greet us.

I assumed the greeter was Richard.

"I am Richard Anthony Fitzgerald III," I figured as much. He looked good as hell. Richard stood about 5'10, athletic build, jet black hair and piercing blue eyes. He looked like may have been in some of those ex curricular activities in college like, rowing or tennis - something with no real physical contact to save his pretty face. That was my guess.

"We would like to thank you for joining us. I've been you all have been caught up with everything with the event and we appreciate you accompanying us," Richard said as we all stood across from each other with him in the middle.

It felt like a middle school dance with boys on one side of the room and the girls on the other side and we're figuring out who's going to pick who.

"Thank you," I said. Stepping forward a bit. He looked at me and his eyes twinkled.

"You must be Penelope," he said, holding out his hand and walking over to me.

"You are correct. Nice to meet you Richard," I said. He was mesmerized. He stared at me like he was in love.

"Nice to meet you Penelope," he said, kissing my hand. "I'm sorry for staring but you are exquisite," he said, making me blush. Not so bad for a rich guy. He seems down to earth, but I just met him so I'm just collecting data.

"Thank you. You're quite handsome, if I must say," I responded. He smiled and looked away. He blushed. This might be an interesting night. "But I'm sure you get that alot,"

'Thank you," he said, stepping forward. "I do, but it sounds so much better coming from you," he said, gazing at me.

"Hmm," I said, raising an eyebrow. He was intrigued. This was going to be an easy night. He turned around to address everyone again.

"I understand that all of you have been matched up so if you please can you find your date for this evening, we can inform you of a bet that we have going on for tonight's event," he stated.

A bet? I was interested, especially if it meant we would get some extra funds for tonight. Everyone dispersed and found their dates for the event and Richard returned to me with a glass.

"Champagne?" he said, handing it to me.

"Thank you, yes," I took a sip and I hated it. I don't know why people drink this shit. It was like licking the inside of a balloon. He was sipping it as if it was some Jack Daniels. It was not.

"So Penelope," Richard said, looking at me. "You are amazingly beautiful. I'm sorry, I didn't expect someone...,"

"Would this look good?" I said, trying to break the ice. He looked a bit nervous.

He laughed, "Yes. I'm sorry, my grandfather set this up. I have never....done....It's usually..,"

"Sorority sisters?" I said and he looked at me. Ding! I was correct.

"Yeah," he said. He relaxed a bit and smiled. "But it can get a little out of hand so we felt it would be better this way,"

"Understandable," I said just downing the champagne. I made a face reacting to the drink and he laughed.

"Not the best tasting drink, I take it?"

"I'm sorry, just not a fan of champagne,"

"It's okay, I have wine. Would you like that?" Richard asked, looking at me and taking my glass.

"Yes please," I responded.

"Come," he said, tilting his head beckoning me to follow him.

Everyone was chatting with each other getting to know their date for the evening. It looked like we were going to have a good ass time. This is the life I never knew about and I was going to enjoy all of this. I would have never thought I would be here a year ago. Shit, Shayla and I would still be having play parties trying to make rent.

And now here I am in a fucking mansion rubbing elbows with the Governor's grandson, like how the fuck did that happen? Vanessa is what happened.

"Okay people, before we go we would like for you ladies to do something for us tonight," Richard stated as he commanded attention. He looked like he was the go-to man.

"Tonight's event will include a charity auction in which we will be auctioned off tonight as for dates," he said and all the girls looked around being intrigued.

"We would like for you to bid on us as your dates," One guy from the side stated as he held Leddy's hand. He looked at her and smiled.

"Yes," Richard chimed in. "What my friend, Bradley is saying is that we want you to bid on us tonight using a credit card we will give you each which holds $100 thousand dollars," he finished.

We all looked at each other amazed. This was going to be a fun night. To spend some money that ain't mine, willingly - hell yeah.

"The guy who has the highest price, will be the winner," Bradley finished.

"Oh nice," I said, taking a sip of wine. It was delicious. Finally something to get me going in order for me to knock off some of these nerves. I guess I was a bit nervous because I didn't know what to expect but I had to remember this was a job and I was prepared.

"Yeah, so I'm gonna need you to spend it all on me," he said, smiling at me.

"So, I get to go on another date with you too?" I asked. I wouldn't mind.

"Of course, would you like that?" He said, reaching for my hand. Richard caressed the back of my hand with his thumb.

"It depends,"

"Oh really? On what?"

"On how you handle yourself tonight," I said, being flirty. I figured I would play on this attraction that was present between us.

"Oooo, I like it," he said softly. He leaned down and whispered in my ear. "I can be bad boy if you need me to be,"

"Mmmm..., how bad?" I whispered back

"As bad as you want me to be," he said softly before kissing my ear. I looked at him and gazed into his eyes. He was fucking gorgeous and he knew it.

"We'll see. I can be bad," I said, tempting him. He stood back and smiled. Richard licked his lips while he stared at me.

"Gorgeous," he said, reaching for my glass. "Shall we?" he said, holding his arm up so I could take it.

"Yes," I said, wrapping my arm around his.

"Ok gentlemen, collect your ladies so we can get this party started," Richard stated loudly. Everyone grouped up and we left in our suvs on the way to the charity event.

Richard held my hand in the back of the suv. He looked nervous and I needed him to keep it together. I held his hand and smiled at him. He gazed at me and blushed.

"Do you mind if I have a request?" he asked.

"What's the request?" I wondered if I had to place a charge. Any additional activities not outlined in the contract would be extra.

"Do you mind if I kiss you?" he asked. I blushed. He wanted to kiss me. That was a first. Just a kiss.

"No, I don't mind," I said, turning towards him. He looked at me and smiled.

Richard slowly raised his hand and caressed my cheek as he leaned in and his lips moved slowly over mine. I could smell the champagne on his breath. His lips were soft and sweet and he kissed me softly. He finished and rubbed his nose against mine.

"Delicious," he said, sitting back still holding my hand.

"Thank you,"

"So how did you become an escort?" he asked. I was not privy to providing my personal information.

"That's a long story and uninteresting. Tell me about being the grandson of the Governor, I'm sure you've seen more than I,"

"I probably haven't seen more, but I've seen something different for sure," he replied.

"True,"

"Well it can be a bit intimidating with the expectations,"

"How so?"

"I'm expected to be a certain way, follow a certain path that has already been planned for me, probably since birth," he said.

"Wow," I never thought of it because I never had rich people's problems. But I guess those born into it, are expected to act a certain way.

"Yeah," he said, looking away.

"Well tonight, you are going to have fun doing what is expected. Your grandfather completed a contract and therefore he is fully aware of the possibilities that could happen tonight," I said, crossing my legs allowing my leg to show at the split. He looked and smiled at me.

"I like how you think," he said, coming in for another kiss. He was a good kisser. I had a feeling I would be calling to process an additional charge before the end of the night.

The charity event went well, and the auction was fun as hell. The guys gave us each a card to 'purchase' them at the auction. Leddy from Humboldt Park won as she paid $55,000 for the guy. They looked like they matched up pretty well too. By the end of the auction, it looked like Vanessa was about to make some money because I saw a lot of additional possibilities happening after this event was over.

"You bought me, now what will you do with me?"

"So when can I have the date?" I asked as I would love to meet up with him again.

"We can have it whenever you want," he replied. "Until then, what will you do with me now?"

"I have a few ideas,"

"Do they include us being naked?" he asked openly. He was ready. Richard saw me and he knew he wanted more.

"They can for an additional fee," I said knowing he was about to make a purchase as well.

"That sounds like a plan," he said, passing me a credit card.

I processed the transaction through my company phone. Vanessa had it all set up, she knew the possibilities and she wanted to cover all bases. We could charge additional services to their contract instantly.

The charge for Richard to have additional services: $3000.00! Paid instantly. As soon as the payment went through my bank alerted me that I received $1500.00 extra. I was satisfied and now it was Richard's turn to be satisfied.

In order for us to complete our night, we had to go back to the hotel on a lower floor as clients are not allowed on the residential floors. Vanessa had rooms that have been designated for such occasions. All of us were fortunate enough to have added amenities therefore we all were able to get paid extra.

Richard followed me into the designated room which was a mini suite.

"Nice place," he said looking around.

"Thank you, but I'm not here for you to look at the place," I said standing in front of him.

"I see," he said, coming in for a kiss and cupping my neck. "Well why don't you show me something to look at," he whispered. I leaned against him and I could feel his growth between his legs.

I grazed my hand over his member and it moved.

"Mmmm...," he moaned softly. "You've awakened the monster," he said as he planted kisses along my neck. I felt him slowly unzip my dress in the back.

"Mmmm,..." I said as I rubbed him as he continued to grow in his pants. " Well, let's see if we can tame the monster, shall we?" I said slowly unfastening his pants as he kissed me deeply.

I had no underwear underneath my dress for such an occasion. I stepped back and removed my arms from my dress and let it fall to the floor.

Richard stood in awe as I stood before him in just stilettos and jewelry. He was speechless.

I came to tame the monster.

Chapter 13 - His & Mine

Mr. Peabody

"I understand the charity event with the Governor's grandson went well, Mr. Peabody?"

"It was Ms. McBride," I answered. She looked stunning as she laid across me naked. The scent of sex filled the air. She had emptied me. My dick was slowly going down, throbbing still from exercising.

"Good," she turned towards me, looking beautiful as ever. Her skin glowed as little droplets of sweat dotted her body. "You were good Brian, as always," she smiled.

"So were you Vanessa," I leaned down and kissed her softly on her lips. I caressed her face as she laid upon my lap looking up at me. Her hair was wild, flowing everywhere. I fucked her senseless and she loved every bit of it as did I.

"I hear that the gentleman at the party had additional activities added,"

"Yes they did. All of them," I answered. She smiled at me and looked away.

"Good girls," Vanessa turned around and straddled me. My dick moved as her canal sat above it.

"I presume so," I said. I slid my hands across her hips down to her ass, grabbing a cheek in each hand. She leaned over and kissed me deeply. I could smell her scent wafting between us.

My dick throbbed as it crossed my nostrils. I squeezed her ass harder as her tongue searched my mouth.

Vanessa started moving her hips slowly back and forth, waking my soldier as he started rising to the occasion.

"I also hear that our girl, Penelope has been awarded a date?" She said steadily grinding down on my rising member. I kissed her beautiful breast as they bounced directly in front of my face.

"Mmmhumm," I hummed and licked her nipple between my lips. She threw her head back and held her titties up for my access. She squeezed them together so I could suck and lick her nipples at the same time. It drove her crazy as I would nibble a bit.

"Oooooo," she moaned as she continued to move her hips around, my member was now on its way to getting rock hard. Vanessa reached back and took hold of my shaft and slowly lowered herself on it; I could feel my dick sliding slowly into her honey pot.

"Mmmhmmm…," I moaned as I looked at her. Her eyes were closed, her mouth slightly opened while she moved her hips in a circle burying my dick deeper inside her. "Again, Vanessa?" I asked.

"You know I can't get enough of you," she said as she leaned forward and kissed my neck. "Are you complaining?"

"Not at all. I always want more of you." I replied, pushing her ass down on my pelvis, shoving my dick deeper inside her. She moaned as I pumped slowly underneath her.

"So tell….mmmm…tell me…mmmm…about…ahhhh," she started. She loved having me inside her. Pleasure roamed throughout her body as she rocked back and forth on me. "Ahhhh...mmmm."

"About the date?" I finished for her.

"Yes....yes....mmm...yes...," She responded. I put my hands on her hips as she sat back and slowed down a bit for us to talk. "I can't talk like this," she smiled. "But I want to know."

"Understood," I said, giving her small kisses on her collarbone. She caressed my head, gently cupping it in her hands. "Apparently, the gentleman had a bet going on,"

"A bet?" She held my shoulder looking at me confusingly. I could feel her doing her kegel exercises to keep me going.

"Ummm,...yeah..," I struggled a bit to speak. I loved the way she felt when she would squeeze my dick from the inside. "The charity event also held a bachelor auction,"

"Interesting,"

"They gave the girls cards to purchase them for charity. The highest bidder was Leddy Gonzales. She purchased her date for $55K," I said as I slapped her ass.

"Oooo, you know I like it when you give me a little pain," she smiled.

"I know,"

"So what about Penelope?"

"Well when the girls bought the guys, they came with a date," I finished.

"Oh, therefore she gets to go on a date with the Governor's grandson." she said, looking like the wheels in her head were turning. "So how were they together?

"He seemed very interested and she played the role well, she may be the one as you said," I said, tipping her chin. "But enough business, I want you here with me." She looked at me.

"Ok," she said as she started moving again. "Everything can't be work,"

"Exactly....mmmm..." I said she started bouncing up and down on my lap.

"You like that?" Vanessa bounced her ass up and down on my dick. I grabbed her ass, holding her down, allowing me to go deeper inside her.

"I love it.....mmmm...I love the way you feel...," I said looking at her. Vanessa smiled and let her head fall back, her hair flowing freely down her back past her ass and tickling my balls like a feather.

"Show me how much you love it Brian." She ordered.

"I aim to please," I said as I pulled her forward and down onto my chest.

I repositioned her legs bringing her knees as far up on the sides of me. Planting my feet directly on the bed and wrapping my long arms around her thighs, I held on to her ass as I thrusted deep inside her from underneath. I fucked hard enough to make her bounce up and gravity pulled her right back down, gliding her pussy down onto my thick cock.

"Uuhhhh.....uuuhhh...uuuhhh....," she moaned loudly as I pounded her harder. I could hear her juices squish as I smashed against her pelvis.

"Mhhff...mmhhhff...mhhff," I grunted. I banged her harder. I couldn't get enough of her. It's something that she does that she does to me that keeps me addicted.

I grabbed her tightly and held on as I rolled her over onto her back with me still inside her. I placed her with her feet on my shoulders because I wanted to bend her over until she breaks.

I slowly watched her as I slid my thick shaft inside her, spreading her wide. She creamed instantly while I stroked her slow and easy. My dick was completely covered in her nectar.

I grabbed her legs, one in each hand and spread them wide as I increased my pace. I loved fucking her and hearing her moan. She enjoyed everything I did for her and to her. She never had a complaint.

"Ooooo....oooooo...aaaaahhh....aaaahhhh....aaaahhhh," she moaned as I started to pick the pace a bit more. I could feel myself getting harder and closer to climax. I wanted to fill her completely with my seed deep inside her.

"Mmmmphff.....mmmpphfff....mmmmmphfff....so good baby....you feel so good," I moaned as I fucked as hard as I possibly could. The headboard creaked as we rocked back and forth on the bed.

"Yes..baby...fuck...it....baby...fuck...meee," she moaned as I drilled her continuously .

"Whose is it?..Huh?...Tell me baby...whose is it?" I asked as I kept stroking her deeply, touching the end of her canal; my favorite spot that makes her wail with pleasure.

Vanessa closed her eyes tightly, holding her mouth open as pleasure rushed across her body while I bang her spot repeatedly. She grabbed her breast, pinching her hard, pebble nipples between her fingers.

"Ffffuuuuuccccckkkk!" She screamed. She was close and I wanted her to tell me it was mine. She already knew it was. Vanessa knew she belonged to me. Just as I belong to her.

"C'mon...baby...mmmmmff," I stammered. She felt so fucking good. "Tell me baby...tell me who this pussy belongs to....tell ....me...," I was almost there. I was trying as hard as I could to keep control but I was about to explode.

"Aaaaa....I'm......I'm.....Aaaaaaaaahhhhhhhhh!"   Vanessa moaned loudly as she reached her climax. I could feel the walls of her pussy pulsating against my shaft making me ride the pleasure train right along with her.

"FFFFUUUUCCCCKKKK!" I released my men deep inside her as I shot my load. "Mmmmhhhh!" I groaned as she grinded her ass against me, draining me completely.

I released her legs and collapsed on top of her. She embraced me fully, wrapping her arms and legs around me tightly.

"That was amazing Brian," she whispered in my ear as she caressed the back of my head. I felt her fingers trail down my back.

I closed my eyes and kissed her on her shoulders while I moved over to lay next to her. She scooted closer and cuddled with me. Her touches were like feathers gliding across my skin as I laid next to her. She kissed my sweat covered chest. She meant the world to me. The smell of our love lingered throughout the room. She didn't admit it, but I already knew the answer.

She knows she's mine.

Vanessa

Brian loves me. I can tell. I know he knows I love him too. We have such a connection, as if we were old souls that were destined to meet. Even though I do what I do, run this company and have my clients, he knows my heart belongs to him and only him. I don't want anyone else. Hell, I don't need anyone else. He completes me fully.

"That was amazing Brian." We had just finished our version of *love* and it was absolutely amazing. Brian wanted me to tell him who I belonged to. He already knew, but I'll never tell. He knows I belong to him, he doesn't need to hear it.

"It's always amazing when I get to be with you," he said as he raked his fingers through my messy hair. We had started just after he had returned home from an errand. He quickly took a shower and came to me.

I know our relationship is not a conventional one, we were not meant to have that. We connect with what we are given and it works for us. Will this advance more? I have no idea and I have never really thought about it. I will always be with him, like I said, I don't need anyone else. He pleases me in ways I can't even imagine. He caters to my every desire and fulfills it, on point. This Bitch has no complaints. And I know for sure, he has absolutely no complaints as well.

He nuzzled me with his nose and kissed me softly on my lips. He scooted off the bed and walked to the bathroom. I watched his sexy black skin shine a blue hue as he walked his naked body back with a towel to clean me up. He walked over between my legs and wiped me clean. Then he wiped himself and placed the towel on the floor. Brian crawled back into bed next to me, sitting up with his back against the headboard.

"Are you happy Brian?" I asked, leaning against his shoulder, looking at him and already knowing his answer.

"Yes, Vanessa. I am happy with you" He tipped my chin giving me a peck on my lips.

"Me too," I smiled. "So now that we are finished playing, we can finish our business." I said looking at him, pulling the sheet up, covering my breasts and his waist.

"Uh, yeah," he focused on my words. "Yeah so Penelope will have a date with Richard III and we will go from there."

"Good, well keep me informed should there be any activities requested after the date," I said thinking about her. "I need to have a meeting with her - here, after the date,"

"Will do," he said, tipping my chin again toward him. He looked longingly in my eyes. "I know you didn't answer my question," he said, glancing at my lips and back at my eyes.

My heart fluttered as he gazed deeply into my eyes, waiting for me to reply to a question that was not asked. He had a hold on me and he knew it. I cared for him so much - I know I did.

"It's okay," he whispered as he kissed my lips. "I already know." Brian smiled.

I knew he did.

Chapter 14 - Unexpected Contract

The charity event was very nice and I had an absolute ball. Richard was nice to hang out with and he wasn't bad in the bed either. Plus I got an extra bonus. I didn't have a problem with that at all. I also was able to go on the date with him, no extra charge. We went to a nice Italian restaurant for dinner at Sierra Tavern in downtown Chicago. It was way out of my league, with or without my job.

We ended back at his place, the mansion, where I was fortunate enough to run into his father, Richard A. Fitzgerald II. He introduced himself while his son was conveniently out of the room.

"Hello there young lady, I'm Richard Fitzgerald II. I'm Richard's father," he said, extending his hand.

I politely laid my hand in his as he kissed the back, "I'm Penelope, nice to meet you Mr. Fitzgerald," I replied. He gazed at me as he lowered my hand from his lips. He looked like he could devour me at any moment. He looked at me as if he was a wolf and I was his prey. The look in his eyes sent a chill through my body indicating he was not the best of people.

"Nice to meet you Penelope," he said, stepping back and looking at me up and down. "I take it that Richard is being a gentleman,"

"He is, thank you for your concern,"

"No problem," he said, folding his arms and tapping the side of his cheek. "If memory serves me correct, you are with Elegant Escorts, correct?" he asked.

He already knew that I was. I don't know what game he was playing but I wanted no parts of it. I'm sure his father set all of this up with him knowing everything his father was doing for his grandson.

"That is correct," I said trying to figure out where he was trying to go with this conversation.

"Interesting, you must be rather new," he said. It was at that moment I realized that he was a frequent customer of Elegant Escorts.

"I am," I responded.

"I figured as much. I would have remembered you," he said looking at me wantoningly. He looked like he frequented the establishment on a regular basis.

"Is there something in particular you're looking for, father?" Richard said as he returned to the living room.

"No," he said, staring at me for a moment and turning to his son. "I was just introducing myself to Penelope.

"Oh ok," he said looking at me and then back at his father.

"Well, I will let you two get back to whatever you were doing," he said walking out of the room. He stopped just before he left, "Nice to meet you Penelope. I hope to see you again," he said looking at me.

"Nice to meet you as well," I smiled. He smiled and left. I looked at Richard who had a concerned look on his face. "Is everything okay?" I asked.

"Yes," he huffed. "I'm sorry, I apologize for my father,"

"Apologize? He didn't do anything,"

"Not yet," he said looking frustrated.

"What do you mean?"

"He always likes to cheat on my mother. I know he uses the service and I knew when he saw you, he would be interested,"

"Oh, I'm sorry,"

"It's not your fault, it's just the way he is," he said sitting next to me on the couch.

"Well, why don't we not talk about him anymore," I said, turning him towards me. I needed him to take his mind off of his father and on to me. "Kiss me," I said. His eyes grew large as he realized what I was saying.

"Won't that be extra?" he asked.

"This one is on me," I said looking at him. Richard smiled as he leaned in for a kiss. He kissed me softly as I leaned back, pulling him with me.

We were in a moment of heavy petting when I realized we were being watched from the hallway by Richard II - young Richard's father. I saw him as young Richard kissed me on my shoulders. I saw him lick his lips from the hallway as he slowly slithered away after getting his dick hard. I was getting a bad vibe about him.

Vanessa

"Hi Penelope," I said as she walked into the foyer of my house. "I'm so glad you were able to meet me at my home,"

"It's not a problem," Poppie said, looking around at the monster of a home. I could see that she was amazed. "You have a beautiful home," she said looking around while we walked to a sitting room.

"Thank you Poppie," I said as she sat down on the couch. "Please sit," I motioned for her to take a seat. She sat across from me while she continued to look around the home.

"Would you like something to drink?" I asked.

"No thank you," she responded.

"Ok, well let us get down to the reason I requested you to come to the house,"

"Ok," she said, turning her attention directly to me. She had grown so much since I found her. She has learned so much and she carries herself with so much more confidence now.

"I understand you had an amazing time at the charity event, is that correct?"

"Yes, it was amazing. All of us had an great time,"

"Good to hear. I love to hear when my ladies have a good time," I said smiling. "I also understand that you also had a date with the Governor's grandson Richard III,"

"Yes, that is correct. Since the event was for charity, the guys participated in an auction. The highest bidder would win a date with their date,"

"Am I to understand that everyone won a date?"

"Yes Ma'am. They gave us credit cards to bid on them," she said.

"Understood, well I'm glad all of you ladies had a good time. The governor was extremely happy with the report he received from his grandson,"

"Well I'm glad, we had a lot of fun together,"

"Speaking of which, I also hear that you were able to meet one of our returning clients, Richard's father - Richard II,"

"Yes, I did," she said, frowning a bit.

"Is something the matter?" I asked about her reaction.

"Well, he's kind of creepy,"

"Yes, he is," I understood what she was talking about. I've heard several comments about him. "He is a bit different from some of our clients. He likes to watch from a distance sometimes," I mentioned. Her face eased a bit after knowing that I knew about his quirks.

"Yeah, he watched his son and I on the couch,"

"He can be a bit weird, but he is actually pretty harmless,"

"Really, I guess it's just the way he stares,"

"Yes, I know exactly what you mean. He stares at you long enough to make you feel uncomfortable,"

"Yes!" she replied. We both laughed. It's nice that she feels comfortable to be open with me.

"Mother," Sam said as he walked into the sitting room. "Oh, I'm sorry, I didn't know you had someone with you,"

"It's okay, Sam, this is one of my employees. This is Penelope. Penelope, this is my son, Samuel," I said, introducing them. I watched as they glanced at each other. Samuel looked at Penelope and was glued.

"Nice to meet you Penelope," he said, holding out his hand. She politely took it and shook his hand.

"Nice to meet you as well Samuel,"

"Please call me Sam," he replied, smiling at her. She blushed and smiled.

"Ok Sam, nice to meet you,"

"Mother, I will be returning late tonight again,"

"Sam, you work so hard you need to take a break," I said. Sam is an amazing son. He never has caused me any trouble. He was like the perfect son. Yet, everyone has a secret.

"I will, I plan on meeting up with some friends afterwards," he said looking at Penelope. He was taken by her.

"Ok, well have fun," I said.

"I will," he said walking backwards out of the sitting area. "Nice to meet you again, Penelope. I hope to see you again,"

"Me too," she said smiling as he left. She glowed as she smiled. Then she realized I was still sitting in front of her.

"Ok well, I have received a request for you directly,"

"For me?"

"Yes. Richard II has requested a date with you. He has paid in advance for additional services,"

"Understood," she said in a serious tone. I liked that about her; when it came to business she was serious and straightforward. She reminded me of myself so much.

"We will set up the date the day after tomorrow. He will pick you up outside of the hotel and you will have dinner and then return to the hotel for the completion of the date,"

"Understood," she said looking at her phone as I sent her the details. "Is there anything I need to know about him?"

"Yes," I wanted to be honest with her when it came to dealing with Richard II. "He can get a bit handsy. And he has been known to get a little rough, do you think you will be able to handle that?"

"Of course, that's not an issue," she said confidently.

"Good. He doesn't usually go further than a bit of spanking and possibly the use of handcuffs,"

"Ok,"

"But nothing more than that," I stated. "Should anything happen out of the ordinary and get out of hand, please contact Mr. Peabody immediately,"

"Ok," she replied.

"Do you have any questions?"

"What exactly does he like to watch?" she asked.

"He likes to watch a woman please herself or he will watch a couple from a distance and please himself,"

"Oh," she said.

"Yeah, he's a strange one to be honest. He will partake in sexual intercourse however it's not always the case,"

"Interesting,"

"Interesting indeed," I agreed. "I have briefed you on Richard Fitzgerald II, do you have any questions or concerns,"

"Not at all," she said smiling. Poppie could handle herself. She had been doing it this long. I'm sure she would be able to handle him and his weird antics.

Poppie

Not only did this motherfucker rub me the wrong way, now I have a date with his ass!

Shit!

As much as I didn't want to go on the date, he paid in advance and it was part of me taking this position. I knew there were going to be some clients that I wouldn't be interested in but this motherfucker I really wasn't.

"I'm not looking forward to this date," I said to Shayla as she sat on my couch.

"I feel you, I have a weird one too. If they pay, I'll play. No matter how weird," she said, taking a sip of her drink.

"Well, hopefully it will go quick,"

"I feel you on that. Nut quick so it can be over," she laughed. I laughed because that was exactly what I was hoping for.

"So when is your date?"

"Tomorrow,"

"Good luck,"

"Thanks, I'll take all the luck I can get with this one." I replied.

Chapter 15 - Unexpected Events

Poppie

Richard II was nice and polite when he picked me up from the hotel. He wasn't acting as weird as he was before, but he was handsy. He loved touching; he liked to slowly run his fingers across my skin just before touching me directly.

He had a good conversation and he didn't cross the line, which I was happy he was behaving. After dinner we ended back at the hotel, in one of the designated rooms. The room was immaculate. It was a suite that provided a view of the lakefront. It featured an office area, living room, kitchen, and a bedroom with a master bathroom.

"Nice place," he said looking around. "You girls get paid well," he said walking around looking at all of the details.

"Thank you," I said walking to the kitchen to open a bottle of wine. I picked a nice year and retrieved two wine glasses from the cabinet.

"Oh let me," he said, taking the bottle and corkscrew.

"Thank you," I said as I turned on the radio to smooth jazz. I wanted to create an atmosphere where I could be alert while fulfilling my duties.

"This is a good year you picked," he said, pouring the wine into the glasses.

"Thank you," I said sitting on the couch. "Care to join me?" I patted the spot next to me on the couch. I wanted to get this over with so I could take a nice, hot shower so I could go to sleep.

As he walked over to the couch, he stared at me the entire time. His eyes were bright and wide as if he was on something but I wasn't sure. All I did know was that he was not sober. He was sweating a bit as he sat the glasses down on the table. I noticed droplets on his forehead and a slight twitch from him every once in a while.

I know this motherfucker ain't come here high! This is going to be one of those fucking nights, I need to really be on guard. He smiled as he sat next to me, placing his hand on my thigh.

"You are so beautiful," he said, taking a sip of his wine as I followed suit. "I see why my son likes you," he finished.

"Thank you," I said looking at him. He leaned back on the couch and swirled the wine around in his glass. He looked at the legs of the wine and then sniffed the glass. He glanced at me and smiled. Richard II took a gulp of the wine and smiled.

He was about to be high and drunk, I thought. Great.

I gulped down my wine and placed my glass on the table. "I'll be back, I'm going to slip into something more comfortable," I said, rising off the couch and heading towards the bedroom.

"Sure, no problem," he said, sitting at the edge of the couch watching me walk away. *This guy is fucking weird for sure*, I thought as I went into the room and closed the door.

I loved the designated rooms because they were not only fully furnished but they were fully stocked with everything we would need to fulfill our duties as an Elegant Escort or Distinct Woman. Vanessa made sure we would have everything needed, nothing was forgotten. So if a lady wanted to change her clothes, the closets were filled with lingerie, gowns, pajamas, in all sizes for all of the girls that worked for the company.

There were only a few girls assigned to specific rooms therefore a girl wouldn't have to worry about the layout due to changing rooms. 3 girls are assigned to a room and the room is booked when the contract is signed. If the room is not ready for the girl, then the date would be moved due to the designated room not being available. This setup is for security measures, if there is a need for one of us to exit the premises quickly.

I returned to the living room and Richard II had removed his clothes, standing in his boxers and socks holding my glass of wine while he was drinking his.

"I heard you coming," he said, holding out my glass, filled almost to the rim. I hope he shoots his load quick, I was not feeling him at all.

"Thank you, " I said while taking a sip. He smiled as I drank the wine. I got nervous as he glared while I drank it.

Did he put something in my drink? I had already swallowed. *Oh Shit!*

I walked past him and set the glass on the living room table.

"Oh my," he said as I turned around. "You are gorgeous,"

"Thank you Richard," I walked over to him and stood in front of him.

He touched my shoulder and traced his fingers down my arm sending a chill throughout my body. My nipples instantly got hard. I wore a cute, light blue nightie which was nipple-less and crotch-less, covered with a sheer light blue robe.

He removed my robe slowly off my shoulders and let it fall to the floor. He stepped closer and I could smell his Old Spice body wash. I smiled because he loved the classics, I loved that smell. He kissed my shoulder softly as his hand found my waist. My breathing altered as I closed my eyes to enjoy his touch.

Richard II kissed along my neck up to my earlobe. He nibbled a bit, sending a spark through my chest, my nipples now pebbles. He carefully cupped my breasts in his hands and squeezed them gently as his mouth moved over my lips slowly. I could feel the stubble from his mustache. He was a good kisser, I thought as I moved my hand over his member. He inhaled deeply as I squeezed his package.

"Mmmmmm...," he moaned, his breathing altered. He slipped his tongue in my mouth tasting mine.

The heat between us began to grow as he kissed me deeply. I slipped my hand inside his boxers and took a hold of his soldier. He was standing at attention. I took him in my hand and began to stroke his shaft.

"Aaahhhh....mmmm...yeah...," he said as stepped back as I stroked him. I kissed his neck and he shuddered. He dick throbbed and jumped in my hand. He was ready to fuck.

"Ready to play, I see," I said.

"Yes Ma'am," he said. He kissed me hard as I tried to walk away to get a condom. "Where are you going?" I stumbled as he grabbed my wrist. My head buzzed a bit.

Did he drop something in my drink?

"I'm going to get a condom," I said looking at him. His eyes were crazy looking again. I didn't like the way he was looking.

Is this what Vanessa was talking about?

Is this why she said if things get out of hand to call Mr. Peabody?

"No need for that right now," he said, smoothing my hair back. "I want you to suck it,"

I looked at him as he waited for me to fulfill his request. I kneeled down before him and stroked his member back and forth. A drop of clear pre-cum appeared as I stroked. I licked it away as I slipped him in my mouth. I cupped his scrotum and slowly sucked him between my lips.

"OH SHIT!" he moaned loudly. He grabbed the back of my head and began to pump himself in my mouth. "YES!....aaaahhhhh,"

I held on to his hips as he steadily stroked himself in and out my mouth. I hoped he would bust his nut in my mouth so it would be over. All I need is one nut and I'm done. He was a nice size as he filled my mouth, saliva dripped out the corners of my mouth as he slowly fucked my mouth. I grabbed his scrotum and massaged them.

"Hmmmmmmmm," I hummed for stimulation.

"OOooo....FUCK....SHIT....aaaaah.......ooooo..," he moaned as I sucked harder and juggled his balls.

He instantly pulled his dick out my mouth and slapped me. It took me by surprise but it was to be expected. I was told in advance. I grabbed his dick and held it as I took it all the way in my mouth and down my throat.

He pulled out again and slapped my other cheek. It was a bit harder but I could handle it.

"I want to fuck your mouth," he said.

"Waiting for you," I said as I slipped my lips over the head of his cock.

He grabbed my head and began slowly fucking my mouth, sliding his cock in and out my mouth. My mouth was filled with his meat as he held the sides of my face, slapping me every so often.

He quickened his pace and held the back of my head as he rammed his mouth down my throat. Tears rolled down from the corners of my eyes as I gagged and choked while he fucked my mouth continuously.

He pulled out and smacked the shit out of me. I knew he was rough, but that I didn't expect. I held my cheek as I knew that would leave a mark. I looked at him and he looked haggard.

"Get the condom," he said as he stood back with his dick rock hard looking directly at me.

I got off the floor and retrieved the condom from the cabinet. I turned around and he was standing directly behind me. It startled me as I didn't expect him to be so close.

"Suck it again," he said. I looked at him and he was swaying.

This motherfucker was plastered. *Shit!* I didn't want to deal with this shit.

Hopefully he will pass the fuck out after shooting his load. I leaned down and took the tip of his head into my mouth. I stroked his shaft and flicked his head with my tongue, awakening his soldier. I opened the package and slid it on the moment he was hard.

I spun me around quickly and bent me over the cabinet, Richard II spread my legs wide and rammed his dick deep inside me in one forceful thrust. Pain ripped through my cavern as I had no lubrication, nor was I stimulated. My tulips burned as I felt a thin layer of skin being ripped as it rubbed against the condom. He began moving in and out as he rammed me from the back. He grabbed my neck and pulled me towards him, arching my back as he fucked me hard against the cabinet.

The side of the cabinet was making an indentation on my pelvis as I was being pressed against is while he fucked me hard. I just needed him to come and for him to do it quickly. I needed this shit to be over.

"You're just a bitch aren't you?" he said. Great, he's a talker. Even better. "Uhh...uhhh...uhh.,"

"Mmmm....mmmm...," I fake moaned. I just needed to play this part to get this over with.

He slapped me hard again. I felt the sting across my face and my lip. I licked the corner of my mouth which caught part of his finger and I tasted blood.

"Take this dick!" he said as he rammed me hard against the cabinet. He squeezed my neck hard to the point I felt my breathing was restricted.

"TAKE IT.....TAKE IT.....TAKE IT...," he said as he continued to slap and fuck me. My face stung with each slap. I could feel the heat on my face, I'm sure my cheeks were red with his fingerprints.

I think I've had enough of this shit. I need to get to my phone and call Mr. Peabody before things get out of hand.

Suddenly, he pulled out and smacked my ass hard. He grabbed my hair and pulled me back towards the couch, me stumbling the entire way.

"Richard II," I started to say as I faced him. "You need to stop!" Richard II struck me so hard across my face I fell to the couch.

I was stunned. This motherfucker just hit me across my face. I turned to look at him, just to see him reaching back and striking me again! I fell to the floor. I had to get to my phone, which was on the kitchen counter in my purse.

I tried to crawl over to the kitchen and he grabbed me and pulled me back. I had nothing to grab but the cushions of the couch which didn't help me at all. I started kicking and he beat my thighs so hard they ached within the muscle.

He stood over me and grabbed my hair, raking his fingers throughout and pulled me to the side of the couch while still on my knees. My mind is going crazy while I feel a trickle of warm liquid on my lip. I touched my lip and realized my nose was bleeding!

I needed to get to my phone.

He grabbed my arms and pulled them back, holding them behind me. He positioned himself forcibly between my legs and rammed his thick cock inside me. I felt violated. I felt this had turned from a sexual encounter to rape. He rammed me hard as he held my arms, pulling me back into him. My face laid directly on the couch, leaving blood on the cushion as he continued raped me.

"You don't deserve my son. You're a filthy bitch! You don't deserve him. You're My Bitch, Now!" he said as he rammed himself in and out of me..

I just wanted this to be over on what seemed like forever. He pulled out of me once again and pulled off his condom. He turned me around and slapped me again, catching me just before I hit the table. Grabbing me by the neck, he sticks his dick in my mouth and rams my mouth. When he realizes I am no longer compliant, shit takes a turn for the worse.

"SUCK MY DICK BITCH!" he yelled and smacked me again.

"Richard II, This is over!" I said, trying to get away. I tried to crawl away and he grabbed my ankle pulling me back. "NO!"

"I PAID FOR YOU BITCH!" he said as he kicked me hard as fuck in the stomach. The kick was so hard, it lifted me off the floor a bit.

It was like in the movies when a person gets kicked in the stomach in an action movie and it goes in slow motion. That's exactly how it felt. It felt like I was in a dream but this shit was happening right in front of me.

"I DON'T GIVE A FUCK!" I screamed as soon as I caught my breath

"YES YOU WILL!" he said as he turned me over and climbed on top of me. He thrust his raw dick deep inside me.

He grabbed my throat and held me as he raped me on the floor against the couch. I grabbed onto his arms as he held and squeezed my throat. My air supply was leaving and he was trying to climax.

I was clawing at his arms, trying to force him to let me breathe as he continued to rape me. "Richard, please stop!" I screamed as he let go of my neck. He instantly hit me across my face. That felt like a fist came in contact with my eye. My vision was blurry in my left eye.

"You're mine Bitch! I paid for you!" he said as he continued. He smacked my face to the opposite side and decided he wanted to change positions.

It was my moment. He was forcing me to get on all fours so he could rape me again from the back. I had had enough. This was not what I signed up for. As soon as he started stroking himself again to get hard, I made a run for it. I ran towards the kitchen counter.

He got up after me in hot pursuit. I reached my purse but he was right on my ass. As soon as I picked up my purse, he pulled me back by my hair and slung me across the room. I fell against the office desk in the room. He quickly walked over and slapped me, spinning me around across the desk.

"Richard," I begged, holding up my hands. "STOP!"

"It's not over until I say it's over," he said as he punched me again. He grabbed my neck and started choking me again.

I looked at him and he looked crazy. He had a wild look in his eyes as he stood clenching his teeth together as he continued choking me. I needed to breathe. I was going to lose consciousness soon if I didn't.

I started slapping him and hitting him, trying to claw out his fucking eyes, but he was determined to make it lights out for me. No telling what he would do to me, once I passed out.

I tried to pry his fingers from around my neck and nothing was working as I started to feel light headed. I was on the verge of passing out and I needed to survive. I wildly tried to grab something off of the desk as he was trying to take the life from me.

My hand landed on something that would get him off of me - quickly.

Stab! Stab! I couldn't stop as he was still squeezing my neck.

Stab! Stab! Stab! Stab! Stab! Stab! I went wild. I needed to get him off of me.

"Aaaaaaaaaaaaaaaaaaaa," he screamed as he finally let me go and fell to the floor.

I dropped the letter opener on the floor and collapsed. He wasn't moving and he was bleeding - bad.

I needed help immediately. This shouldn't have happened. I crawled to my purse and got my phone to call Mr. Peabody. I was dizzy as it was hard to see the screen.

I dialed Mr. Peabody. I was going down.

"Hello?" I heard Mr. Peabody answer the phone.

"Help," I whispered.

Chapter 16 - Aftermath

Samuel

My mother is Vanessa McBride, the Notorious Madame of Chicago. She earned that name due to her running and escort service. I don't understand the big deal about it though. It's not like she is doing anything wrong, yet many people say that my mother is the head of an exclusive prostitution ring. I find that hard to believe. It's just an escort service.

I know she means well, as she's just trying to find partners for everyone, even those that may be socially awkward. She even has it out for me; she's always trying to find someone for me. I know she wants me to have the perfect mate, but I think I would be the judge of who would be perfect for me.

There was one person who came over to the house not long ago who piqued my interest. I thought she must be extra special because my mother had her over to the house. She hardly ever has any of her employees over to the house. The only one would be Peabody, but I know he's not just an employee - he's my mother's lover and significant other.

They may think I'm gullible and blind but I see how they treat each other and how they speak to each other, that is way more than an employer-employee relationship. He's been around for about the last 5 or 6 years, working for my mother and keeping her happy.

I like him, he's good for her and he's a good person all together. I know he's younger than her, not much older than me but when it comes to them, age is just a number.

"So how's it hanging, Peabody?" I said as I walked in the kitchen door. He was chopping vegetables along with having the counters filled with pantry items. "What are you about to make?"

"Dinner for your mother and I," he said as he threw the veggies in the saute pan. "I've been doing good, how about you?"

"I'm good. But I need you to tell me straight up, who is the chick that my Mother had over the other day?" I asked.

He looked at me as if he was contemplating telling me a lie. He shook his head and continued chopping the vegetables. "Her name is Penelope," he finally answered.

"Yeah, that's the one. What's up with her? Why did Mother have her at the house?"

"She had a special project for her to handle,"

"Really? Must be someone high profile," I replied.

"Very," he said as he stirred the veggies sizzling in the pan. I watched him as he added garlic and pineapples and bell peppers.

"What are you making again?"

"Sweet and Sour Chicken," he replied as he added the sauce to the mixture. The aroma coming from the pan filled the entire kitchen.

"Did you make enough to share?" I asked, hoping to get a taste of this wonderful smelling meal.

"I'll leave some for you," he said smiling.

"That's my guy. I know you won't let me down!" I said, giving him a 'pound' across the counter.

He turned off the stove and poured the sauce over some breaded chicken and gave them a little toss. His phone rang on the counter just as he was pouring the meal into a large serving dish. He looked at his phone and immediately picked it up.

"Hello?" he said, looking concerned. "I'll be right there, don't touch anything!" he said as he disconnected. "Looks like you can eat first, I have to take care of something very important," he said quickly leaving the kitchen.

"Oh ok. Next time I'll ask you more about that Penelope girl," I said as I grabbed a bowl to dig into the meal. "I think she's cute." I said to myself as my mouth watered looking at the meal before me.

Mr. Peabody

"Vanessa," I said as I drove over to the hotel. "There has been an incident,"

"With whom?" she asked.

"Penelope,"

"Is she okay?"

"I'm not sure, I will let you know as soon as I arrive and analyze the situation," I said.

"Okay, keep me posted," I disconnected the phone. I didn't want to tell Vanessa and get upset before I had eyes on the situation. But from the sound of Penelope's voice, it didn't sound good.

I arrived at the hotel and took the private elevator up to the designated floor. I opened the door and instantly saw that everything was not exactly - okay. The place looked as if there was a fight and nobody won.

I saw Penelope on the floor and rushed over to her. She had bruises all over her face, her eye was swollen shut and she looked as if she had unwillingly participated in forceful sex acts.

"Penelope? Can you hear me?" I said leaning down close to her mouth. She slowly opened her one eye and looked at me.

"Mr. Peabody," she strained to say as she reached for me.

"It's okay Penelope, I'm here. Everything will be okay," I said, trying to get her off the floor.

"Richard...he....he...," she started crying as she tried to tell me what happened.

"I know, Sweetheart and I'm so sorry. Let me get you out of here first and I'll take care of him," I said as I picked her up off the floor and she instantly passed out.

I laid her on the couch while I tended to the Governor's son. He was bleeding pretty bad and he hadn't moved since I arrived. I checked his pulse, it was faint but still present. I had to take precautions and activate the emergency plan for Richard.

"Hello, yes this is Peabody. I need two teams on the designated floor #2, room 711, immediately," I said.

We have procedures that I follow when situations arise, especially with our high profile clients. Therefore we have cleaner teams for every situation possible, even death. In this case, we need two medical teams - one for Penelope and one for Richard. I will work on the damage control once they have been removed from the scene.

After about 10 minutes, the cleaner team and two medical teams arrived to analyze the situation. A cleaner team is always dispatched for any situation.

"Take Mr. Fitzgerald to Mount Sinai Hospital and call his assistant once you have arrived," I said pointing to one team. They immediately started working on Richard checking his vitals.

"I need the remaining team to load up Penelope Matthews. Make sure she stabilizes and hold on for a moment for further instructions," I said as I walked towards the door. "I need to make a quick phone call," I had to call Vanessa.

"Brian, I thought you were going to eat dinner with me," she said, pouting over the phone. I love when she misses me.

"I know, but there has been a situation,"

"A situation? What happened?"

"It looks as if Richard attacked Penelope," I said, shaking my head. Penelope didn't deserve it.

"Oh my goodness, how is she?"

"Not good. She took some pretty hard hits, and it looks as if he may have..." I didn't want to say it. It made me so angry just thinking about it. I care for each and every lady that works for Vanessa and this is something that rarely happens, but when it does it makes me sick to my stomach.

"Oh my. Bring her here, to the house. I will call my doctor. She can be set up in the south wing," she said. She will make sure Penelope has the best care.

"On our way," I said, disconnected. I stepped back into the room and the first medical team was ready to move out.

"Take the private elevator at the end of the hall," I said and they left with Mr. Fitzgerald.

"Vanessa would like for Ms. Matthews to be taken to the mansion as she will have her specialist tend to her there," I said and the medical team took Penelope on a stretcher out the door and down the hallway to the private elevator.

The cleaner team was quickly at work, cleaning the designated room, making sure everything was tidy and neat.

I left them to finish up as I was no longer needed in the room. I had gathered Penelope's items and headed downstairs to the security office.

"Hey Peabody, what it do?" One of the guards said as I entered the office.

"Hello gentlemen, it's good, it's good, you know how it is," I said, smiling at them.

"What can we do for you today?"

"I am going to need a copy of the security footage for Room 711, Designated Floor #2,"

"Awww shit," the other guard said. "Why can't people act right?" he said, pulling up the footage.

"Is there a particular time?"

"From 6 pm on, I need everything copied and sent to me immediately. " I said as I walked to the door.

"It's on the way," Guard #2 said. "I hope everything is okay,"

"It will be." I said as I left.

I arrived at the mansion shortly after the ambulance. Vanessa met the ambulance outside as it pulled into the gate. Sam had come out with her. I wish he hadn't. I know he was just asking about Penelope and now he will be more concerned than ever if he sees her like this. Before I could get out of the car fast enough, he and Vanessa were at the back of the ambulance as they opened up the doors to pull Penelope out.

"Oh my, Penelope," Vanessa said as she covered her mouth. Sam held his mother as they took her out of the ambulance.

Sam just stood beside his mother in awe as they wheeled Penelope into the and down the corridor to the south wing. Vanessa walked over to me looking for answers.

"Did she say what happened?"

"No, she was out of it. He beat the fuck out of her Vanessa," I looked at her.

She knew I was upset because of my past, that was something that I swore to never do - hit a woman. No matter how angry a woman may make me, I will never raise my hand to hit her. I had seen enough when I was younger with my mother and father. My father would beat my mother senseless to the point she would be knocked out for hours.

"I know," she said, caressing my cheek. I closed my eyes to control my anger. "Did she try to protect herself?"

"Yes, she did. She sent him to the hospital," I said, sounding like a proud father. Penelope took care of herself. She wasn't going down without a fight.

"Good for her, I will deal with that in the morning. But for now, we need to make sure she is taken care of," Vanessa said walking back into the house.

"What happened, Peabody?" Sam said, looking for answers.

"She was attacked," I answered. He looked concerned and worried about her. "She'll be okay, she's a fighter. She sent the person to the hospital,"

"Good. I hope she'll be okay,"

"I'm sure she will," I said, putting my arm around his shoulders as we walked back into the house.

This was just the beginning of a shit storm that's coming since this was the Governor's son.

Chapter 17 - Legal Matters

Vanessa

"This makes no sense," I said as I walked from the south wing of my house to my office. I had to get ready for the storm that was brewing. Mr. Peabody entered as I looked over my files for the Governor. "Good, you're here. Can you tell me what happened?" I said looking at him searching for some kind of answer.

"It looks like Richard attacked Penelope and raped her as well," he said trying to hold it together. I knew this was something that he hated to deal with when it came to the ladies. It hasn't happened much, but it has happened.

"Oh my god," I said, covering my mouth. "Was she able to give you some information?

"No, she was pretty much out of it Vanessa. He beat the fuck out of her," he said tearing up. I could see just him talking about it disturbed him.

"Understood. Did you request the security footage?"
"Yes,"
"Good, you know the procedures," I said. He nodded and left the office. Sam entered shortly after Mr. Peabody left.

"Mom, how's Penelope?" he asked. Sam amazed me. He had only met her once and he was already concerned about her. I knew I had made the right choice.

"I'm not sure Sweetheart, the doctor is still examining her. As soon as I find out, I will let you know," I said walking over to him.

"She was so nice. Even though I only met her for a short time, she seemed nice. She didn't deserve this,"

"You are correct, she didn't. I'm sorry you had to see her like this," I said looking at him. "She'll be okay. I'll make sure of it,"

"I know you will Mom, you take care of all of your employees,"

"I try,"

"Will you keep me posted on Penelope?" he said as he started walking towards the door.

"Sure," I said, curious about his interests in Penelope. I didn't want to push the issue therefore I let it go. "I'll let you know as soon as I hear something."

Sam left me alone in the office. As I sat down at my desk, I looked over the file for Richard Fitzgerald II. He had been a client of mine for quite some time now, but it wasn't in the past few years that a pattern had started to form with him. Going over his file, he had an incident in which he attacked another one of my ladies about 8 months ago. This was around the time in which I was informed that he had to get help for substance abuse. From the looks of what happened tonight, he had fallen off the wagon.

My phone rang and startled me a bit. I looked and realized it was Mr. Peabody calling.

"Yes Mr. Peabody," I answered.

"The media outlets have caught wind of it," he said quietly.

"What are they saying?"

"The Governor's son has been rushed to the emergency room with life-threatening injuries,"

"Understood. Thank you, " I said, hanging up the phone.

It was getting late and shit was building up. I should expect a call from the Governor's office in the morning as well as Richard's lawyer.

Normally in certain situations such as these, a normal person would be nervous and worried about the outcome. But I'm not as normal as one would think, I made sure to cover all of my bases therefore when shit hits the fan like this, it just slides right off.

I was working in my office when the doctor came in to give me an update on Penelope.

"Hello Dr. Davis, how is she?"

"She's taken a beating Vanessa," he said, sounding concerned. "Luckily there are no fractures to her face however she is extremely bruised and her eye is swollen shut with minor damage to her eye,"

"Oh dear god,"

"It should heal, however I will check it to make sure she still has vision in that eye. As far as fractures, she has a few broken ribs. I can only assume she took a few blows directly to her chest," he said looking at his paperwork.

"Will she be alright?"

"Yes, she will eventually recover, however she will need time to do so,"

"Thank you Dr. Davis, she will have all the time she needs,"

"I've given her a mild sedative to allow her to rest for the remainder of the evening. Would you like a nurse to come in the morning to help her?"

"Yes Doctor. Can you please make sure the person you send understands that this is a sensitive matter and to keep it confidential?"

"Of course Vanessa, it is totally understandable. I will also have them sign an NDA as well,"

"Thank you, I appreciate it," I replied.

"Vanessa, can I ask who did this to her?"

"Richard Fitzgerald." The doctor knew him well as this wasn't the first time we had to tend to someone who had a contracted date with him.

"Him again? He went ballistic this time,"

"I see he did. At this point, I am ready to cancel the contract with Richard II as he didn't learn from the last time this happened,"

"I completely understand. I will send the nurse over in the morning," he said as he stood up to leave. "Call me if anything should change with her, but she should be out for the rest of the night. She needs the rest, honestly."

"Thank you Dr. Davis, I appreciate you coming so quickly,"

"It's okay, anything for you Vanessa," he said as he left. As soon as he left Brian entered the office.

"How are you?" he asked.

"I'm tired of Richard,"

"I understand. Everything has been taken care of,"

"Thank you. I will need to speak to our lawyers tomorrow as a result of this. In the meantime, were you able to get the cleaners into the unit as soon as possible?"

"Yes. They arrived shortly after the medical teams. The security cameras have also been reset as well."

"Thank you Brian," I said leaning back in the chair. "I noticed that Sam was concerned about Penelope, did you notice?"

"Yes I did. He asked about her earlier before I got the call,"

"He did?" I said getting excited about some good news for a change.

"Yes, he asked about her,"

"Interesting," I replied. Just then I received a text message regarding Richard II. "It seems though the media is reporting that he is out of emergency surgery and is intensive care,"

"How would you like to handle it this time?"

"What we will do is wait until any allegations are brought up and then we will more forward accordingly,"

"Understood," Brian stared at me. He knew me so well. He knew I had a lot to deal with and I didn't expect something like this to happen again and to a new employee as well. It was not my intention of having that happen to her or any of my girls.

"Vanessa," he called me in his serious tone. I know what that meant.

"Yes," I said looking at him.

"C'mon," he said, holding out his hand. Brian was taking me away from the matter at hand as there was nothing more than could be done at the moment. "Let's get dinner,"

"I really don't feel like cooking and I've sent the staff home already,"

"I've already taken care of everything," he said. He usually does.

"Ok," I said, taking his hand and walking out of the office. I'll deal with this shit tomorrow.

Tonight, I wanted to enjoy the calm before the storm.

Vanessa

After meeting with the lawyer, I had full confidence that everything would go as planned. I waited patiently for word from the Governor. However, I was very surprised when I received word the Governor wants nothing to do with this matter and requested that it be put to sleep quietly. I had no problem with that. He knew exactly how to handle this situation; to remove himself from it as it could get really ugly.

His son, Richard II, refused to go away quietly. His lawyers contacted me as soon as I entered the office; they were waiting to speak to me.

"Hello Gentlemen," I said upon entering my office as they sat in the front office. "You may follow me,"

I walked into my office, followed by two of Richard II's team and Mr. Peabody. I sat down at my desk as Mr. Peabody came and stood beside my desk looking at the two sitting in front of my desk.

"How can I help you gentlemen today?"I said.

"We have some legal matters to discuss regarding Mr. Fitzgerald, which should be kept confidential," A lawyer said looking at Mr. Peabody.

"Mr. Peabody is my assistant and he will remain present in this meeting, as he is fully aware of anything and everything that has to do with this company," I said looking at both of them. "He will remain in this office during this meeting otherwise, this meeting is over."

"Understood." They folded like lawn chairs.

"We would like for you to produce the individual who entertained Mr. Fitzgerald on the evening of the incident," One of the lawyers said, pulling out what I can only assume was the contract between Richard II and Elegant Escorts.

"I'm so sorry as it seems as though you have made a useless visit to the office as that information will not be provided to you,"

"Well, we are prepared to take this matter public and shut this place down," The other lawyer said with a bit more authority.

They threatened me. One should *never* threaten me.

I glanced at him and he swallowed hard. Apparently, he had never dealt with me and my company before so I went easy on him. Richard II knew better than to send me fresh meat to try to intimidate me. I smiled as I looked at Mr. Peabody who passed me a manilla envelope. I opened the envelope and glanced at the contents of the package.

"Well again," I said, closing the envelope and looking at both of them. "I'm sorry for you having to come all the way down here, but there was a breach of contract which was outlined as before,"

"Yes, however in this case, your employee sent Mr. Fitzgerald to the hospital!" The second one was getting heated. He was really trying to earn his paycheck.

"I understand this. However, it was your client, Mr. Fitzgerald who created the incident therefore he breached the contract which resulted in him being sent to the hospital," I retorted.

"Understood, however he is in intensive care,"

"Through no one's fault but his own," I replied. "He also sent my employee to the hospital as well. As a matter of fact, she has not awakened as of today," I said and the both of them looked at each other.

"Um, well uh," The intense lawyer replied. He was not prepared for the information which was probably not provided to them.

"Gentlemen," I said standing up and picking up the envelope. "I can only assume that by your reactions, you were not informed that she needed medical attention as well," I walked from behind my desk holding the evidence.

"That information was not provided to us," The mild lawyer stated.

"Of course it wasn't," I chuckled as I stood before them. "Listen, this was not the first time we have had to deal with Mr. Fitzgerald and his lawyers when it came to him and his actions during a contracted date," I looked at both of them squirming in their seats.

"We are aware of his past incidents, however those were settled out of court. This will not,"

"On the contrary, it will," I said, passing them the envelope. "Mr. Peabody, can you please grab me an espresso please?" He nodded and proceeded to the beverage station on the opposite side of the office.

I watched as they opened the envelope and examined the contents. Both of them looked at each other and began collecting their things.

"We need to evaluate and discuss this matter more thoroughly with our client and will contact your office thereafter,"

"Understood," I said as they rose from their seats. "I look forward to hearing from you,"

The lawyers left quickly with their tails between their legs. I figured Richard II didn't tell them exactly what happened due to sheer embarrassment. They may have been recently added to his legal staff and totally not aware of Richard II and his antics.

"They were not prepared," Mr. Peabody said as he brought me the espresso.

"No they weren't. Richard knows better than to send amateurs to me,"

"Especially since this isn't the first time with him," he said.

"Exactly."

Chapter 18 - Awake

Samuel

I went and checked on Penelope when I returned. I saw the nurse leave her room and I slowly opened the door to her room. She was awake watching tv.

"Hi," I said as I entered the room. She turned towards me, trying to focus with her one eye as the other was still swollen shut.

"Hi,"

"How are you feeling?"

"Like shit," she said looking around. "Where am I?"

"You're at the mansion, well my house. My mother had you brought here after your incident,"

She looked around at all the medical equipment and then at herself. She slowly touched her face, cringing as went over her injuries.

"I must look awful," she said, looking away and pulling up her bed sheets.

"No, never. You are still as pretty as the day I met you," I said. Penelope looked at me and I smiled.

"No I'm not," she said, tearing up.

"No, you are. This is just temporary," I said walking over to the side of the bed. She smiled and looked away.

"You're sweet. Thank you,"

"So do you need anything?" I pulled over a chair next to the bed to take a seat and have a conversation with her.

"Not that I know of," Penelope's stomach growled loudly. She looked at me to see if I had heard it.

"You sure about that?" I asked, chuckling.

She smiled and covered her mouth, "Okay. I may be a little bit hungry," Penelope smirked looking at me. She was beautiful. I saw her as she was when I met her. Red hair flowing down her shoulders, freckles spotted across her nose, soulful eyes and a smile as wide as the sea.

"No problem, I'll grab you something to eat. Is there anything you can't eat or don't like?" I got up and pushed the chair back so I could go to the kitchen to find food for Penelope.

"Um, no I don't think so," she said closing her eye as she tried to think.

"Okay, I'll be back," I left to grab her something to eat.

I met Mr. Peabody in the kitchen while I grabbed a variety of things for Penelope to eat. I wasn't sure of what she could eat but I wanted her to have options just in case there was something that she couldn't eat or didn't like. I grabbed random foods like cheeses and fruits, yogurt, crackers, meats and some broccoli and cheese soup leftover from yesterday's dinner.

"I see you are a bit hungry, you doing a mukbang?" Mr. Peabody asked as I gathered everything on a tray.

I chuckled as I looked over the tray, " Ah, naw. This is for Penelope, she's awake."

"Is she? How is the feeling?"

"Her words - like shit,"

"I can imagine, she's been through a lot in one fucking night," Peabody took a deep breath and shook his head. He doesn't like violence of any kind but this one hits home for him.

"Yeah, so I wasn't sure of what she wanted or what she could eat, ya know due to...,"

"Yeah, I know," he looked at me and then at the tray. "Well it looks like you have a good selection. Probably add something to drink?" Peabody said, walking over to the fridge and grabbing two bottles of water and two bottles of Naked Blue Boost.

"Yeah, thanks,"

"I'll help you," he said as he motioned me to pick up the tray.

We walked back to Penelope's room, Peabody opened the door for me to enter. I walked in and placed the tray on the side table next to the bed.

"Wow, that's a lot of stuff,"

"I wanted you to have a bit of everything," I said as I took the beverages from Peabody.

"How are you feeling?" Peabody said, walking over to the side of the bed. She reached out and grabbed his hands, cupping them within hers.

"I'm okay I guess. I feel like shit but I'm here," she said.

"That you are,"

"I want to thank you Mr. Peabody....for helping...me..," she started getting choked up as spoke.

"It's okay," he interrupted. "I'm glad you called me and you're safe now," he said, sitting on the side of the bed and comforting her.

"Thank you though, I really appreciate it,"

"No problem," he replied.

"But why am I here and not in a hospital?"

"Well, Vanessa is very picky and private. She wanted to get you medical attention without having to answer questions about your injuries. She has the best doctors who have a residence with the local hospital however they are also on our payroll," he said. *Mother had a lot of fucking hookups*, I thought.

"Oh, well I can see why," she said.

"I'll let you two back at it and I will let Vanessa know that you are awake. She would want to know," he said, getting off the bed and walking towards the door. "I'm glad you are on the mend,"

"Me too," I said. Penelope and Peabody looked at me. I just stared back at her. She blushed and looked away.

"Good night," Peabody said as he left the room.

"So, I got you a bit of everything. Nothing needs to be kept cold so it can stay in here with you. But I suggest you eat the soup as that won't stay hot,"

"That sounds like a plan," she smiled at me.

I helped her with propping up the pillows behind her so she could sit up with minimal pain. She winced as she moved slowly and carefully into position while holding her stomach. She was in pain and there was nothing I could do to take it immediately away. Once she was situated, I gave her the soup.

"This is amazing, you bought this?"

"No, Peabody made it?" Penelope's eyes widened as she looked at me. "He cooks too?"

"Yeah, he does a lot. He is a man of many skills," I said.

I had a great time talking to Penelope. She got a bit of food in her and she seemed in good spirits. I didn't want to keep her too long as I had other things to tend to and I wanted her to get some rest. She was happy that I came by to see her and asked me to come back tomorrow. I most definitely will.

Vanessa

"Penelope is awake," Brian stated as he entered the living room.

"Really? She must be hungry," I raised up off the couch to head for the kitchen.

"No need, Sam has brought food in for her," I looked at him, raising my eyebrows.

"Really?"

"Yes, he's been asking about her,"

"Yes, I am aware. And he took her food?" I said smiling. My son was caring for someone; someone who I had chosen for him.

"Yes. He took a variety of things to eat,"

"Interesting," I said as I grabbed my robe and headed towards the south wing.

As I approached her room, I could hear Sam and Penelope talking softly. They were just making small talk, but I enjoyed that he took it upon herself to check on her. I softly tapped on the door to announce my presence.

"Hello?"

"Come in Mom," Samuel said, pulling open the door. I walked in and Penelope tried to adjust herself in the bed.

"Hi Poppie, how are you feeling?" I asked. She smiled as I knew she liked when I called her by her nickname.

"I'm good, thank you for everything," I walked to the side of the bed and held her hands.

"You are most welcome. I'm sorry this happened to you. I feel responsible for all of this shit that has happened to you,"

"Don't be, you didn't know he was going to do this, besides how could you know?"

"I should have canceled his contract long before,"

"It's okay, really. I'll bounce back from this, trust me,"

"Such a brave girl," I said, smoothing her hair back. I looked at her and she smiled.

Poppie smiled even after all of the shit she just went through, she still held her head high. I'm so proud of her.

"I'll say," Samuel chimed in.

"I am concerned a little though,"

"About what?"

"I stabbed him," she said as she looked down at her hands. "I needed him to stop." Tears fell slowly down her cheeks.

"I know. You did exactly what you needed to do,"

"But I don't want to get you in trouble," she looked at me for reassurance. I smiled.

"No worries Poppie, everything is being taken care of. His contract has been canceled due to breach of contract and we are dealing with it legally,"

"Are you sure?"

"Positive." Poppie looked at me and seemed satisfied.

"Well, I see that you are good hands with Sam, so I'll leave you two,"

"Oh you don't have to go,"

"It's okay, I wanted to come and check on you, but my son has been the perfect gentleman, therefore I know you are in great hands."

"Yes she is," he quipped.

"He has been very helpful and has been keeping me company. He brought me all of this food," she said pointing to the tray with a smorgasbord of food.

"I see. Did you leave anything in the kitchen?" I joked. Samuel rolled his eyes while she giggled. It was nice to hear her laugh. It made me feel as though she will actually be on the mend.

"Well, I will leave you two now. Please call Mr. Peabody if you need anything. I'll come around to check on you periodically but I will get updates from Sam," I said looking at him.

"Thank you again Ms. McBride," Poppie said as I headed towards the door.

"No worries. You just get better," I said walking out the door.

Chapter 19 - Need to know

Samuel

I left Penelope to get some rest shortly after my mother left. I didn't want to keep her up and there were places I needed to be. I prepared myself before going out by smoking a nice blunt in my room. I called my buddies and told them that I was leaving out.

Mother knows about my condition. She understands. Yet sometimes I don't, but yet I do. It's complicated and only for those that are like minded understand. It's basically the reason why she tries so hard to find someone for me. She feels I need to find someone who can handle me - *period*.

As I arrived, I noticed the parking lot was damn near full. It was nice to get away from the house and into my element. I sat in the car and watched a few people walk into the establishment. This is a private, members only club which is very exclusive for those who live this lifestyle.

I approached the door and flashed my member's card and the retractable queue lane was removed from the blacked out door. The doorman opened the door as I walked into a dimly lit room while he closed the door behind me.

"Good Evening Mr. McBride," The gentleman behind the front desk said as I handed him my jacket.

"Good Evening Mr. Peters, how are you doing this evening?"

"All is well Sir,"

"Good to know." I walked through the only red door in the room and entered a long hallway with doors marked with names - last names. I walked down to my usual room, displaying 'McBride' on the door. I swiped the keycard and entered the room.

I flicked the lights on to display a bed in the middle of the room covered in black satin sheets. Above it, a sex swing with straps and handcuffs. Along the side of the walls were bondage contraptions as toys were displayed on a corner storage unit. I had come to play again tonight as I have in the past few years.

After my shower, I waited until my first participant arrived. Mother knows about my fetishes and as we had a deep conversation when I was younger. That's why she is always trying to find someone compatible with me. I understand her concern, but I feel I need to be the one to find the perfect companion that will be able to accept me as I am.

Dressed in my boxer briefs and my satin robe, I lit a pre-rolled joint while waiting for my playmate of the evening. I usually accommodate one or two participants depending on how I feel; tonight I will have a repeat playmate.

As I inhaled deeply on the joint, there was a simple tap at the door. I opened the door to a masked individual by the name of Debbie.

"Hello," she said in a sultry tone of voice. I stepped to the side to allow her to enter.

"Hello yourself," I said as I closed and locked the door behind me.

"I'm surprised you responded to my text message. You have been a hard person to catch up to McBride,"

"I've been distracted. But I'm here now and that's all that matters," I walked over to her and stood behind her as she stood near the bed.

I moved her long red hair off her shoulders to reveal her lovely, elongated neck. I kissed her neck softly as she mewed a soft moan. She laid her head to the side as I nibbled along her neck while pulling her closer to me. I felt my member awake as she grinded her ass against my pelvis.

"Mmmm, I see that you remember me," she said as she groped my soldier between my legs.

"I always remember you," I said. "Stay in one place," I demanded as I walked away from her. Debbie stood still while I grabbed a blindfold to cover her eyes.

I blindfolded her and removed her coat to show her dressed in a black, lace lingerie two piece outfit with straps holding her nylon stockings.

"You've been a bad girl," I said as I noticed she missed a strap. I pulled on the strap and released it as it popped back against her. "You didn't complete your straps," I whispered in her ear.

Her breathing altered as she inhaled as she moaned softly. "I'm sorry, I thought," she began to speak. I pressed my finger across her lips to stop her from speaking.

"No talking," I whispered in her ear. She nodded. I walked over to the storage and grabbed nipple clamps and placed them on her protruding buds. This was her first time having them on so I watched as she winced in pain.

"Are you okay?" I asked as I didn't want her feeling uncomfortable with anything I'm doing. She didn't answer. She obeyed me well. "You may speak,"

"Yes, I'm fine," she enjoyed the pain. She slightly opened her mouth to accept the feeling of pressure upon her pebbles. I kissed her hard, searching her mouth with my tongue. She cupped my head which was incorrect. I grabbed her hands and held them behind her while I continued kissing her. "Naughty, naughty," I said, stepping back while still holding her wrists behind her.

I grabbed a pair of handcuffs, placed them on her wrists and raised her arms above her head. I connected a hook to the handcuffs that hung from the ceiling.

"I'm...," she started, then hesitated.

"No talking," I grabbed a paddle and gave her a tap on her precious ass cheek.

"Aaahhh,..." she moaned as she stood with her ass turning a slight pinkish red at the point of contact.

"You like that? Huh?" I said as my member stood at attention. Her moans turned me on. Just the thought of her moaning beneath me turned me on.

"Yes," she moaned.

"No talking." I tapped her again.

"Aaah...aaahh," she moaned again.

"You like that, don't you?" I waited to hear her respond, she didn't. "Speak,"

"Yes, please,"

"Please what?"

"Spank me," she requested.

"Naughty naughty," I said, walking around and standing in front of her. "Open your legs,"

She obeyed as she stepped with one foot to the side, leaving her legs agape. I pulled her panties to her ankles. "Step out," she obeyed.

As I knelt in front of her, looking at her hairless muff before me. I held her hips as she opened her mouth waiting in anticipation of my next move. "Don't come." I demanded as I buried my face between her legs, my nose resting at the top of her mound.

"Aaaa.....aaaa....aaaaa," she moaned and wiggled as I flicked her folds quickly with my tongue. I tasted her nectar as I continued to lick across her clit.

"Hmmmmmmmm," I hummed as I closed my lips around her clit. Her knees buckled as I sucked her slowly. Her legs began to shake as she began sitting on my face. I gave her two pats on her ass cheek which jolted her to stand up straight as I continued pleasing her.

"I....aaahhh...I....," she moaned as I sucked her juices. "I'm....I'm...aaaa..,"

"Naughty, naughty," I said as I stood up before her and kissed her, spreading her juices over her lips. I gave her ass cheek a harder spank, which made her back arch. "I said, don't come,"

She turned her head towards me, her mouth open as I padded her ass again. Her head hung back as she bent forward a bit as if asking for another spanking.

"You like it don't you?" I said as I padded her again. She moved with pleasure each time the paddle came in contact. "Speak,"

"Yes!" Debbie moaned as I continued to paddle her ass until it glowed red. Freckles dotted her body as I removed her bra, setting free her twins and leaving the clamps still attached. I pulled the chain that connected them and she wiggled with pleasure. "Ahhh....mmm,"

I removed the cuffs from the hook, lowering her arms, yet holding her wrists in front of me. I looked at her as she stood before me, her flawless skin glowed in the yellow hue of the room. I caressed her face and kissed her gently. I held her head in my hands as she lowered her hands and squeezed my member.

"Permission to speak," she whispered close to my ear. I could feel her breath dance across my lobe.

"Speak," I said as I kissed her across her cheek softly to her ear lobe, sucking softly. She moaned softly while I continued kissing down her neck and across her shoulder.

"Permission to please you, Sir," she spoke as she slid her fingers along the top of my boxers.

"You want to please me?" I said kissing her across her chest above her breasts.

"Yes, Sir, please," she begged.

I flicked her nipples with the clamps; she shook and moaned with painful pleasure.

"Yes, please me," I granted her wish. A smile spread across her face. She lowered to her knees while holding my waist.

Debbie slowly pulled down my boxers, my soldier popped out and hit her forehead as she removed them. She grabbed a hold of my shaft and began stroking me slowly. I closed my eyes as I felt her take me into her mouth as her lips wrapped around my manhood. I felt suction as her tongue flicked my head.

"Uhhh….mmmmm, good girl," I said as I held her head and began stroking her mouth. I could hear the sloshing in her mouth as I entered, filling her mouth completely. Debbie was very good when it came to her mouth. She knew exactly how to please a man.

I pulled off the blindfold to reveal her green eyes looking back at me. Her red hair flowed down her back as she took me in and out her mouth. I was almost ready to explode as she continued to suck me hard as I pumped her mouth. I could feel my shaft growing harder, I wanted to feel her before I exploded. I pulled out of her mouth immediately leaving her wanting more.

"Please, did I do something wrong?" she said bowing down while still on her knees.

"No. Stand up," I said; my cock still standing at attention. She obeyed and I led her to the bed by the cuffs. "Lay down," she laid on her back on the bed. "Spread them,"

She spread her legs wide as she waited anxiously for me to enter, her *flower* - pretty and pink as could be. As I stood at the side of the bed, she reached and grabbed my shaft and stroked me again. I watched her as she motioned me to come inside her. I grabbed a condom, slipped it on and granted her wish.

Chapter 20 - Threats

Vanessa

As I thought, Richard II would not go away quietly. The media covered his condition as him being attacked while out at a charity event. And of course media channels were present at the event therefore pictures of the attendees were readily available.

I hadn't made it into the office soon enough as the phone rang rapidly. Photos of Richard II and Penelope were plastered everywhere. Every news media channel displayed her face as well as a moment when they stood together for a picture before entering the event. People were calling as they found out that Penelope was an employee of the Elegant Escorts. That just started another firestorm all by itself.

"Good thing you had Penelope sent to the house instead of the hospital, they would have been all over her," Mr. Peabody said as he sat in front of my desk.

"I know, I thought this shit would blow over by now, especially since the Governor doesn't want anything to do with it.

However, it seems as though I now understand why he decided to distance himself, " I said looking over the files.

My phone rang from the front office.

"Yes?" I said as I pushed the speaker button.

"Ms. McBride, Lawyers of Mr. Richard Fitzgerald II is here within the office to see you," I rolled my eyes.

"Let them have a seat, I'll call you when I'm ready," I said and disconnected. I pulled open the drawer and pulled out two aleve pain pills. Mr. Peabody fetched me a glass of water to take the pills.

"It looks like we have to go to phase 2 Mr. Peabody," I said as I downed the last pill, throwing my head back as I swallowed.

"Really?"

"Yes, it seems as though Mr. Fitzgerald is trying to play hardball," I said as he tapped on his tablet. "His lawyers have arrived. I can only assumed that they are here to serve legal papers,"

"I agree. I will make sure everything is set up and wait for your call," he said as stood and walked towards the door.

"Thank you. On your way out, can you send them in please?" He nodded as I prepared myself for Richard's attack.

Mr. Peabody held the door open as 3 well dressed men walked into my office. All of them carried briefcases and one handed me an envelope. I hesitated to take it as I knew they were trying to serve me legally.

"Hello Ms. McBride, we meet again," One of the lawyers said as he sat down in the open chairs in front of my desk.

"Hello Mr. Ruiz. And yes we meet again,"

"Consider yourself served," he said as I took the envelope from him. "You are being named as a defendant along with your employee Penelope Matthews in the attempted murder of Richard A. Fitzgerald II," he said looking at me with a smirk on my face. I looked at the others and they all had the same silly smirk.

This didn't bother me at all and yet they were examining me to see if I would break a sweat. Not even, apparently they were not prepared for me. I remembered Mr. Ruiz from our last meeting when dealing with Mr. Fitzgerald. After that incident, I took precautions to make sure that it does not happen again. Especially with Mr. Fitzgerald as he was a high priority client who had the backing of his money to do his talking for him.

"Interesting," I said, examining the documents. "Gentleman, it seems as though you have your information to move forward," I said, raising my eyes to them.

"Yes we are," Another lawyer said. "If you are willing to settle out of court, we are prepared to negotiate, however, it needs to be reasonable,"

"I see. However, settling on behalf of my company is not acceptable as we are not at fault here. Therefore, we will go to court if need be, yet I highly doubt it,"

"How can you say this? Your employee attacked Mr. Fitzgerald and put in the hospital. Are you aware of this? Or do you leave your lackey to handle tough situations for you?" he quipped. I shot him a cold stare which made sit up straight in the chair.

"What is your name?" I asked, pointing directly at him.

"Mr. Young," he answered.

"That you are," I said standing up behind my desk and straightening my outfit. "You see Mr. Young, I've been in this business a very long time. And being in this business for a very long time allowed me to learn from my mistakes and in doing so I've become confident in my business and my employees,"

"Yes, but that doesn't make you above the law," he retorted. I looked at him. He interrupted me.

"Penelope Matthews accompanied Mr. Fitzgerald that evening and we were informed by him that she was his attacker," Mr. Ruiz stated.

"And this is what he told you?"

"Yes. Where is your employee? We are prepared to have her arrested immediately for attempted murder," The final lawyer chimed in.

"She is unavailable," I answered. "Unfortunately you will not be speaking with her nor will she be turning herself in,"

"Then you will be held liable," Mr. Young said. He made me smile. I chuckled at his attempt at intimidation.

"You think so?"

"Your prostitute will go to serve time for this and you, Ms. McBride, will lose your company. Do you know who you are dealing with?" he quipped. I looked at him and smiled.

I turned to Mr. Ruiz. "He's really working for his money today, huh?" Mr. Ruiz kept a straight face and nodded.

"On the contrary Mr. Young, it is *you* who doesn't know who you are dealing with. I don't take kindly to idle threats. In fact, I don't take kindly to being threatened, period,"

Mr. Young huffed in his seat ready to speak.

"Excuse me," I said, raising my finger to them. "Who is the lead prosecutor on this?" I asked.

"That would be me," Mr. Ruiz answered by raising his hand.

"Ah, thank you," I responded. I dialed out to Mr. Peabody.

"Mr. Peabody, could you please send that information to Mr. Ruiz, one of Mr. Fitzgerald's lawyers please. Just the first portion," I said, disconnecting the call.

Soon after disconnecting, Mr. Ruiz received a message from Mr. Peabody. It was a video recording of the night in question. It wasn't the entire video, but just enough for them to get an understanding that this will never go to court. He will settle out.

"Mr. Ruiz, what you have received is a partial video of the evening in question. Please let me know what you see," I said as he looked at his phone and began playing the video.

My blood ran cold as I heard Penelope scream in the video and then it went silent. I closed my eyes as my heart went out to Penelope having had to deal with that type of situation. I looked at Mr. Ruiz and he looked disgusted.

"One moment, Ms. McBride," he said as he sent the video to the other lawyers. I sat down at my desk and waited for a response, especially from Mr. Young.

I watched as his mouth opened and he looked very uncomfortable watching the video. He looked at me and had nothing to say. Shortly after, I received a video chat - from Mr. Richard II himself, from his private hospital room.

"Vanessa," he said as he struggled to keep the phone steady.

"Yes Richard, I hear you loud and clear. How can I help you?" I said looking at him on my laptop.

"Vanessa, can we discuss this?"

"Richard, I thought that was what you had intended on doing, however you sent your lawyers after me. You know Richard, how I don't like lawyers," I said looking at Mr. Ruiz and giving him a wink.

"About that," he stammered.

"I take it that you didn't disclose the events that happened with them,"

"That girl stabbed me!"

"And she had every right to, you attacked her," I replied.

"I will not stand for this Vanessa. You need to do something about those savages you call employees,"

"Richard, now you know I've told you before, you are not to address my ladies that way," I said. I could see he was getting upset as I was not backing down at his antics.

"I will sue you Vanessa,"

"It was a binding contract to which you breached, we've been through this before Richard. Now either you settle out of court and pay the amount for breach of contract, plus additional fees in the amount of $10 million plus have your membership revoked, and I will let this go away quietly,"

"And if I don't?" he asked. I looked at his lawyers who just shook their heads.

"If you don't, the full, unedited version of that night will be sent to every news channel and social media platform. I suggest you discuss this with your lawyers,"

"You wouldn't dare," he said looking at me. I leaned into the screen to make sure he saw my face clearly.

"You should know by now Richard, I don't play games. Especially when it comes to my business. You want to try and find out? You will suffer the consequences,"

"Give me the girl, Vanessa and I'll go away quietly," he tried to bargain.

"That will never happen. I suggest speaking with your lawyers and get back with me. And do not try to intimidate me again Richard. I don't like being threatened," I stated.

"This isn't the end of it Vanessa!" he yelled as I closed the laptop.

"I suggest you speak with your client and get him to realize the consequences of his actions. Otherwise, this video and the fact that he tested positive for methamphetamines will be released to the public," I said, looking at Mr. Ruiz who understood everything I was saying.

"How did you know about the meth?" A surprised Mr. Young asked.

"As I said before Mr. Young, this is not my first rodeo. I've been in this business for a long time and it is best when you play this game, you hold all of the correct cards in order to win the game. Please let Mr. Fitzgerald know that he will also be banned from Elegant Industries as well," I said smartly. Mr. Ruiz smiled in agreement.

"Thank you Ms. McBride for your time," Mr. Ruiz said as he stood, with the others following suit. "We'll be in touch,"

"I look forward to hearing from you soon." Mr. Ruiz nodded, turned and left the office with the other two lawyers following directly behind him.

Mr. Peabody returned shortly after the lawyers left and sat down at the desk. I looked out the window at the skyline. I hoped Richard II was smart enough to take the deal.

"Do you think he'll pay?" he asked.

"He should, but with him on the drugs again, he's not thinking rationally. I don't want to get involved in it like this. I don't want Penelope hurt because this asshole doesn't want to admit he did wrong,"

"I know. Hopefully someone will knock some sense into him,"

"I agree. In the meantime, I need to make sure we are ready to roll if needed. I'll let Penelope know what may happen." I said.

"Understood."

Chapter 21 - Caught Wind

Mr. Peabody

A few weeks after the meeting with the lawyers, Vanessa expected to get a payout from Richard II. It would have been logical for him to do so. But like most rich people, who don't want to part with their money, he decided to take matters into his own hands and act - *stupid*.

Sam had come back from taking care of his things that he usually does on Monday, Wednesday and Fridays. He was home a bit early this time, as she seemed a bit frustrated.

"Wassup Samuel? You look irritated,"

He exhaled deeply, "I'm good Peabody," he said walking into the kitchen and taking a drink out of the fridge.

"You don't sound convincing,"

"Bruh," he sounded stressed. "It's just...," he wanted to say it but he thought too much about the subject. He shook his head and looked at me.

"Wassup," I leaned against the counter waiting with a listening ear.

"Mom's right dude, I need to find someone," he finally blurted out.

"Interesting," I responded. Sam had been against his mother trying to find someone for him and it was interesting to hear him say that he needed someone. He's always been a loner only because he hasn't found the right person whom he can be open and honest with, therefore he does what he does.

"Why'd you say that?"

"I never thought you would agree with your mother. So you found someone from the club?"

"No, not exactly," he said looking at me. I was curious as to who may have piqued his interest for him to agree with his mother.

"What do you mean?"

"It's complicated," he said, finishing his drink. "I don't know how this person feels about me or anything at the moment,"

"Oh," I replied. I looked at him and he had a serious look on his face. He had been in deep thought for a while. "Well take one day at a time. Find out about the person and then find out their interests. They will eventually give a hint if they are interested in you, then go from there," I advised. It was the best I could do.

"Yeah, I could do that,"

"Why the change of heart all of a sudden? Are you going to tell your mother?"

"Well, it was after my last....," he stopped and looked at me.

"I know. Go ahead," I reassured him that we didn't need to go into details too much. I already knew about his extra affairs.

"Cool, well it was then I realized, I couldn't do it forever. I want to find someone that understands me,"

"I completely understand," I said thinking about Vanessa. "You will, trust me. Who knows, you may have already met her," I said as my phone rang. He looked at me and his eyes widened?

"What do you mean?" he asked. I held up my finger to have him wait as I answered the phone.

"Wassup, Peabody here," I intensely listened to the person on the other end who had given me some very stressful news. Apparently, I wore it on my face as Sam looked concerned as he waited for me to respond.

"Is that so?" The information I was receiving was not expected and I felt that I needed to take the matter into my own hands. "Thank you for letting me know. I'll handle it from here." I said and disconnected the phone.

"What was that all about? What will you handle from here?"

"Nothing you need to worry about. I will inform you in due time. Are you planning on going back out tonight?"

"Nah, why?"

"I need to handle a few things and I need you here at the house should I need to call back here,"

"Peabody, what is going on?" He looked worried.

"I just got some intel and I need to check it out before jumping on it," I said, scrolling through my phone.

"Oh ok, well I'm in for the night and possibly the weekend. I think I'm gonna give myself a rest,"

"That sounds like a plan. How about you go and check on Penelope? She might enjoy seeing you,"

"You think?" he said, perking up. It was then I knew why he wanted to stop. He wanted Penelope.

"Yeah, I think she enjoys your company," I said, boosting his ego.

"I think so too. I'll go and see how she's doing," he smiled and walked in the direction of the south wing.

I headed towards my room to check on a few things before I informed Vanessa of what was discovered.

By the time I had verified everything, I had to inform Vanessa to make her aware of what was going on. She needed to know so she could figure out what our next step would be as I needed the next few steps coordinated in order for me to keep Vanessa safe.

"Vanessa," I said as I opened her bedroom door. She was brushing her hair at her vanity table, looking as beautiful as ever.

"Yes Brian," she said, turning around and looking at me intensely. "What's wrong?" She knew immediately by the tone in my voice.

"I don't want to alarm you,"

"What is it Brian?"

"A hit has been placed on your head." Vanessa looked at me and stood up with her mouth agape.

"Are you serious? How did you find out this information?"

"One of the guys let me know. They told me none of them wanted to take the job, but one newbie did," I told her.

"A newbie?" She stood in front of me. "By who?" she asked, looking at me. I didn't want to tell her but I had no choice. She was going to be pissed.

"Richard II." Vanessa's eyes widened and then she frowned so hard, I knew she was beyond pissed.

"This motherfucker had the nerve to put a hit out on me because of this fucking lawsuit!"

"Seems like it,"

"Brian, how much is to be paid out?" She wanted to know how much this man wanted to pay to have her killed.

"Is that important? It's not going to happen," I said, standing straight with my hands clasped together in front of me. I was ready to go to war.

"How much, Brian?" Vanessa demanded.

"1 million." I said. She looked at me and I watched the anger take over her eyes. She was ready to make heads roll.

"Are you fucking serious? He is willing to have me killed for a million dollars just so he won't have to pay $10 million that he fucking owes me. Well now he owes me interest," she said walking over to her laptop.

"That's understandable," I said, walking over to her. "You don't have to worry. Nothing will happen to you,"

"I know you will make sure that I'm okay, but who will protect you?" she asked.

"Now you know, I can take care of myself,"

"Yes, but I don't need you dead trying to protect me,"

"You ain't getting rid of me that easy," I said, sliding my hands around her waist and pulling her towards me.

"C'mon now, this is serious. How are we going to handle it?"

"You let me do all of the work," I kissed her forehead and led her to the bed. "I don't need you to worry, you focus on the next step since Richard II wants to play games. In the meantime, I'll handle the hit,"

Vanessa sat on the side of the bed, holding onto my hands. She was worried, more so about me than herself. I didn't want to tell her that I knew when and where the hit was going to happen as I didn't want her to always be on alert. I needed her to relax and go with the flow. I hated keeping her in the dark, but it was best for her own good.

I tipped her chin up and placed a loving kiss on her lips. I lingered as she cupped my face in her hands. She pressed her forehead against mine as I held her hands.

"Brian...," she hesitated. She was scared and she didn't want to show it.

"I got this. Trust me," I said looking in her eyes. "I won't anything happen to you, I promise." Vanessa looked at me and caressed my cheek. She gave me a weak smile and nodded in agreement. "I'll be back," I said as I planted a kiss on her forehead and left.

I needed to handle some business. They messed with the wrong person.

Vanessa

Brian just informed me that Richard II has paid someone to kill me. This is something that I didn't expect and I will not take lightly. Apparently, he was not happy with the terms of the settlement, therefore he figured the best way to have it go away was to get rid of me.

Wrong move! I see that Richard II wants to play hardball, well he has threatened the wrong person. I know Brian can take care of protecting me, but I'm worried that he is not thinking about having protection himself. I'm sure he can handle almost anything but he is not bulletproof.

While Brian was out doing what he does best, I decided to plan my next move. Since Richard II didn't want to pay me willingly, I'll have to force him to do so. I hadn't planned to release the videos to the public but he left me no choice. I will have to prepare Penelope about what may come out. My plan was to keep her out of it as much as possible; however, with her being with Richard II the night of the event, it's inevitable that the news media will place Penelope as the individual in the video, even if she's blurred out.

I walked to the south wing to speak with Penelope and heard her speaking with Sam. I smiled as I loved the fact that he enjoyed speaking with her. I tapped softly on the door and waited for a response.

"Come in," she sang. I opened the door to see Penelope sitting on the side of the bed smiling, looking better than ever.

"Hello Poppie, how are you?"

"I'm good. Feeling better, thank you. I should be able to get back to my apartment soon," she said, folding her legs upon the bed.

"In due time, no rush," I said sitting down on the bed next to her. "Poppie, I need to talk to you about a few things,"

"I'll let you two talk. I'm gonna go and take a shower. I'll come back before you go to bed, if you like?" Samuel asked.

"I would like that," Poppie smiled. She likes him, I thought. I knew I could have been a matchmaker in a past life.

"Great, see you then," he said smiling as he left the room.

"What is it you need to talk to me about?" she said, turning her attention towards me.

"Unfortunately, I need to talk to you about the night of the incident," I said. Poppie's facial expression dropped. She didn't want to relive it and who would?

"I figured we would have to speak about it, eventually. It's okay…I've been thinking about it honestly,"

"What have you been thinking about?" I asked.

"How I could cut that fucker's balls off and feed them to him." Poppie blurted. She looked at me with such anger in her eyes. She had been hurt and she wanted him to hurt just as bad. I agreed.

"My kinda girl," I said. She looked at me, surprised that I agreed. "I knew I liked you," she smiled and I wrapped my arms around her as she leaned in for a hug. She wrapped her arms around me and I held her for a moment just taking in the moment.

"How can we do that?" Poppie said sitting up and wiping away tears that had fallen down her cheeks.

"Well, I found out that in order to hurt sadistic rich people, you have to know how to hurt them,"

"What does that mean?"

"Some rich people are great to have as friends because they are about helping others as well as increasing their wealth. Whereas there are a handful of rich individuals that don't give a shit about anyone but themselves, yet they want everyone to know about them,"

"So how do we humiliate him?" she said. She was smart and she caught on quickly.

"Unfortunately, that's where you come into play. I'm not sure if you are aware, I have video of the entire incident. Copies have been made, with your identity blurred. However, it was already known that you attended the event with him, therefore people will eventually put two and two together."

"You're wanting to release the video," she said. I looked at her and nodded. She stared at me for a second and then down at her hands.

"Yes. But only if he doesn't agree with the settlement terms."

"Settlement terms?" She looked confused. "I don't understand."

"We have been meeting with his lawyers due to a breach of contract. Therefore we are looking to settle out of court with a few terms and conditions. Along with a $10 million dollar payout, half going directly to you." Poppie's eyes grew large as saucers.

"$5 million dollars?" she stammered.

"Yes. It is part of the contract everyone signs when they become a client. Should they breach the contract in any way, it is a cash payout with a minimum of $2 million. It may increase depending on the breach."

"Wow."

"In this matter, we are requesting $10 million dollars and we will revoke his membership. He will not be allowed on any premises under the Elegant Escort Corporation." I finished. She looked amazed.

"You are one bad bitch," she blurted. I laughed so hard, I couldn't contain myself.

"I'll take that as a compliment."

"It was," she said looking at me. "So how do we do this?"

"I will have to release the video to the media networks and social media platforms, only after he pays in full."

"And if he doesn't?"

"Oh, he will." I said looking at her. "Will you be alright once it is released? You may be contacted by a few reporters and such. I will do everything I can to make sure it will not disrupt you in any way."

"I'll be fine. I want this motherfucker to suffer." she said scooting further in the middle of the bed.

"So do I. And I will. I promise."

Chapter 22 - Minor Distractions

Mr. Peabody

After I had caught wind of the hit put out on Vanessa, I knew I had to stay with her everywhere we went. I knew it would happen, I just didn't know when or where. I was glad that my *'people'* told me about the contract otherwise there would be no need to be on guard as Vanessa usually does not have anyone threaten her just because of who she is.

Vanessa was irritated that Richard II hadn't paid out on the settlement and with a contract on her head, she was irritated that she couldn't speak about it to anyone. With his lawyers still on hold with the settlement I felt she needed to relax and I knew exactly how to take her mind off of everything.

After dinner, Vanessa and I decided to spend some time together in the living room. I opened a bottle of wine as she stood at the fireplace watching the fire. She was in deep thought as I offered her a glass.

"Thank you Brian," she said as she took the glass and took a sip. "I don't understand why he just doesn't settle instead of trying to have me killed."

"Well, the way I see it, if you were dead, he wouldn't have to pay the money, the video wouldn't be released and his reputation would remain intact."

"That motherfucker gets on my last nerve," she said as she took another sip. I wanted her to relax and not think about him. The conversation was not going in the direction I wanted as I intended for her to relax so I had to take matters into my own hand.

"Well me ease your tension," I said as I came up behind her and kissed the back of her neck.

Her body relaxed as she tilted her head allowing me better access. I turned her around to face me and looked lovingly in her eyes. I cupped her face in one hand and kissed the side of her neck again. She moaned softly as she enjoyed my touches. I slipped my hand around her waist as I pulled her closer to me.

"Brian, I...," Vanessa started. I placed my finger across her lips.

"Shhh," I whispered. I removed my finger and planted a kiss upon her lips. She quickly relaxed and submitted herself fully to me.

I kneeled down before her in front of the fireplace and lifted her nightgown to reveal her lace panties. I slipped them down her legs as she slowly stepped out of them one foot at a time. She held the top of my head for balance as I raised one leg and placed it on my shoulder giving me access to her sweet spot.

I moved in closer and planted a kiss on her mound. She looked down at me as I opened my mouth to enjoy her nectar. As I flicked my tongue between her fleshy folds, she held my head in place as she pressed her vajayjay against my mouth. I sucked her juices as she grinded against my mouth.

"Oooooo.....aaaa.....ooooo," she moaned softly.

"Mmmmmmmmmmmmmmm," I hummed against her mound as I flicked her clit.

"Ooooo shit Brian,.....that feels so good," she moaned loudly.

All of a sudden we heard someone in the hallway. Someone must have seen us and left quickly as we both heard movement outside the living room and then a shadowy figure could be seen leaving the area.

"Brian," Vanessa said, tapping me on the top of my head.

"I heard it too," I said, raising my head.

"Let's take this to the bedroom," she said. I agreed.

Even though we were interrupted, my mission was accomplished - Vanessa stopped talking about Richard II.

Now, all I needed to do was to put her to sleep.

Poppie

I was so grateful that Ms. McBride has allowed me to stay at her mansion while I recover. She didn't have to but she knew what would happen had I stayed at a hospital. I had been in contact with Shayla and she was telling me that there were reporters everyday at the building trying to catch me coming or going so they could bombard me with questions about what happened with Richard II.

Staying at the mansion had its perks for sure. I got to meet Samuel, Ms. McBride's son. He reminded me of someone but I couldn't put my finger on it. He was so nice to me the entire time I stayed here. Samuel would come and talk with me for hours and bring me food while checking on me daily. And he was fine as hell to look at. I wondered if he had someone special.

I decided to take a walk around the mansion, since I had been cooped up in the room for a few weeks. I really needed a change of scenery. The mansion was huge and it seemed as though I was on one side of it. I decided to try and find Samuel's room to pay him a visit. I must have walked all over the fucking place before I saw a light glowing from what was the living room.

I figured someone would be there as I'm sure they wouldn't leave a fire burning. As I walked slowly towards the living room, I saw Ms. McBride standing near the fireplace with a glass of wine in her hand. I was just about to approach her as she put the glass on the mantle and began to moan.

I stopped in my tracks, hoping the darkness of the hallway would mask my presence. It was then I realized that she wasn't alone. Mr. Peabody was kneeling before her as he placed her leg upon his shoulder, burying his face between her legs.

Mr. Peabody and Ms. McBride were getting it on in the living room!

Just watching them made me intrigued as I wanted to continue but I didn't want to be a perv. The way he was making her moan made me realize that I had never had someone to make love to me. I've been fucking around with all of these people but never made love to any of them. As I watched them, I could see the passion between them. He took his time to make sure he pleased her.

I slowly tiptoed away, still keeping my eyes on their foreplay and not paying attention to my surroundings; resulting in me bumping into a planter in the hallway.

"Shit!" I whispered loudly as I caught it just before it hit the floor to reveal my presence. I hurried back toward the direction from which I came hoping no one heard me.

Back in my room, I thought about how Mr. Peabody was pleasing Ms. McBride and how she was really enjoying him. As I laid on my bed, I closed my eyes and tried to mimic what she was feeling as I began to masturbate. I wanted to rub one out as I hadn't had an orgasm in a long time since the incident. I kept my eyes closed as I pinched my nipples while I rubbed my clit in circles with my fingers.

"Mmmmm...," I moaned softly as I began to move my ass while I opened my legs wider for better access to my love cavern. I hadn't noticed that I had left my door slightly cracked open while I pleased myself in bed.

"Hey Poppie," Sam said as he entered the room and startled me. "Whoa,"

"Oh my goodness," I said. "You scared me,"

"I'm sorry, I didn't mean to. I see you're...um...I'm sorry, I'll let you go and ...," he said, turning around to leave.

"No, wait," I said. "You don't have to go,"

"But, um...you were...um," he said pointing at the bed.

"I know," I said sitting up. "You caught me,...um....,"

"Yeah. It's cool though, we all do it," he said smiling. I blushed and giggled nervously.

"Well, I can tell,"

"What do you mean?"

"Well, I came looking for you, but I couldn't find your room," I said as he closed the door and sat on the bed facing me.

"You came looking for me?"

"Yeah, you always come to check on me, I wanted to return the favor." Samuel smiled shyly.

"That was nice."

"Yeah, if I had found you. But I got lost and....," I hesitated in telling him about his mother and Mr. Peabody.

"And?"

"Well, I kinda ran into Mr. Peabody and Ms. McBride...in the living room...," I stammered.

"Oh," he said, his eyes widening. "You must have seen them getting busy,"

"So you know?"

"Yeah, they have been at it for a while now. Be careful as they will get busy anywhere and everywhere around the mansion,"

"Oh wow," I said. "Well, I kinda watched a bit," I said, wincing a bit.

"Oh," he said, raising his eyebrows. "So that was why you were....um...,"

"Yeah. I'm sorry, I know I sound like a perv,"

"You don't actually,"

"Really?" I was shocked he was okay with me spying in on their escapades.

"They love each other, even though they aren't willing to admit it,"

"I think it's nice to have someone to make love with,"

"You don't have someone?" he asked. I smiled at the thought that he would think I would have someone.

I shook my head from side to side. "Unfortunately, I don't. Besides who would want to be with me," I said looking down at my hands. Samuel reached over and held my hands. I looked up to meet his gaze.

"I would." he said confidently. I didn't know how to respond.

I looked at him and he was serious. He smiled, making me blush as he moved closer to me still holding my hands.

"Are you...,"

"Serious? I am." he interrupted me. He nodded. My stomach flipped. "If you will have me,"

My mouth hung open as he smiled at my reaction. "Of course," I managed to say.

Samuel moved closer and my heart felt like it was about to break out of my chest. As he got closer, he kept his eyes on me. I closed my eyes as he planted a kiss on my lips. His lips were warm and full as he slipped his tongue in my mouth.

My secret garden quivered. I wanted him. I wanted him badly. He kissed me deeply as he held the back of my head ever so gently. He pulled back and looked me in my eyes.

"When you're ready, I want you. I want to make love to you, the way you are supposed to be made love to." he said softly as he caressed my face.

"I would love that," I said, caressing his face and smiling. "But at my apartment."

He chuckled. "I completely understand. I'll wait for you," he said, holding my hands and kissing them.

"Thank you, Samuel."

"The pleasure is mine."

Chapter 23 - Time's Up

Vanessa

Things seemed to have gotten back to normal and Poppie had recovered and moved back to her apartment. Mr. Peabody made sure security was beefed up as we didn't need any incidents on the property as reporters would still try to catch a glimpse of Poppie. Poppie hasn't been assigned to anyone at the moment as I wanted her to go through therapy first.

I had a long meeting for the day which kept me at the office longer than I had expected. After work, I had dinner plans at a local restaurant in which Mr. Peabody accompanied me. Dinner was amazing and it was nice to be outside of the house enjoying the evening with him. We haven't had an evening together in a while; we usually have dinner at home because he loves to spoil me with a home cooked meal, which he does rather well.

"You know, I'm happy we came out tonight," I said as we walked out the restaurant hand in hand.

"I'm glad we did too," he said, kissing me on the forehead. Brian opened the umbrella so we wouldn't get wet while we walked to the car parked in the parking lot across the street. "I still think you should have waited for me to get the car so you wouldn't have to walk over to it."

"It's all good Brian, it's just across the street. Besides, I'm with you, I feel safe," I said as he wrapped his arm around me.

"As you should," he said. We walked quickly across the street before the traffic raced down the street. The pavement was wet from the misty rain and to be honest, it seemed really quiet. A little too quiet. I looked at Brian for reassurance and he carried a stern look upon his face; he looked down at me and smiled, easing my anxiety.

Brian unlocked the car remotely just before we reached the car; suddenly everything seemed to go in slow motion. Brian reached for the door and a car pulled up quickly into the parking lot, drawing our attention.

It stopped directly in front of our car and a door opened. Brian pushed me into the car and I heard a gunshot.

POW!

The car door window shattered into a million pieces. I covered my head and buried myself on the floor on the passenger side. Brian covered me with his body as the guy kept shooting.

POW! POW!

Two more shots rang out and hit the windshield. I looked at Brian as he kneeled down behind the passenger door. The shooter wasn't a really good shot but he was still shooting randomly. I saw Brian take off his coat and grabbed his gun from his waist in the back.

It had gotten quiet. Again. Too quiet. The car was still there because I could hear the music blaring in the night. I could hear police sirens off in the far distance, it would be a minute but they were coming. Then it happened.

Brian stood up after seeing movement off to his side.

POW! POW! POW! POW! I heard about 3 or 4 shots go off and saw Brian take a few as he stumbled back towards the car.

Brian got shot! My heart dropped. Not Brian. Not my Brian.

POW! POW! POW! POW! POW!

More shots rang off. This time it was Brian responding. He caught his balance leaning against the car and shot back at the driver. The driver fell to the ground and didn't move. Brian stood up holding his stomach and walked over, his gun still drawn and stood over the guy.

POW!

Brian unloaded one last shot to his head. Brian struggled to turn the guy over, checking his pockets to find anything on who he was. I'm sure he was the contract killer that was hired for me.

"Brian!" I screamed practically falling out of the car to reach him. He was stumbling back to the car, he had been hit a few times and he was bleeding out badly. "No! No, no, no, Brian!" I said as he fell to his knees right as I fell and caught his head on the way to the ground.

"Please! Somebody! Help!!!" I screamed to the top of my lungs. A few waiters who were outside smoking cigarettes on the side of the restaurant ran over after hearing me scream. One immediately pulled out a phone and called 911.

"Brian, stay with me baby, please. Don't leave me, Brian!"

I can't do this without him. I wouldn't want to. He was my heart.

Poppie

It was nice to be back at my apartment. I hadn't gone back to work yet, because Vanessa wanted me to have some therapy, which was fine by me. The last time I had some sort of therapy was back at the foster facility where they kept kids who were about to age out of the system.

I had finally got up the nerve to invite Samuel over to my place. It had been a while since we had seen each other, since I left the mansion. We've talked on the phone and videoed each other but nothing more than that. It seems a bit strange and new to me because I have always gotten physical with someone and then found out about them. With Samuel, it's been different.

I think he's holding back something but I can't put my finger on it. I'm confident I'll find out in due time. He's sweet and caring. He loves calling me 'Poppee' with more emphasis on the ending. He also has a little, weird facial expression that I remembered only one other person doing the same thing, which makes Samuel look so familiar to me.

He arrived at my door, on a rainy night, where I had just ordered some chinese food. I opened the door thinking it was my order but I came face to face with Samuel.

"Hey Poppie," he smiled while I opened the door to let him in.

"Hey Samuel, I thought you were my chinese food," I said looking down the hallway. Just as I was about to step back in the door, the delivery person came around the corner with my food.

"Perfect timing," he said as he saw me grab the food and close the door.

"I know right. You must be hungry," I joked.

"Actually I am, but I was going to offer to go out to eat," he said, watching me stride to the kitchen with my food. "I was going to ask you to come join me along with my mother and Mr. Peabody, for dinner."

"Oh, I'm sorry, I didn't know,"

"Maybe next time, we can always eat with them," he said, coming into the kitchen.

"Your mother is an amazing woman," I said, opening the bag and taking everything out, placing them on the table.

"Yes she is," he said, helping me by opening the containers. "She's special. When she saw me she said she knew I was the one she wanted."

I looked at him confused by what he said. "Wait, what?" I blurted. He snickered and looked at me.

"I'm adopted. My mom adopted me when I was very young, I think about 4 or 5 years old," he said as I placed several items on a plate in front of him.

"Really?" I said looking at him. "I would've never guessed. To be honest, I thought you were product of a divorce,"

Samuel laughed, "No, it's just been me and my mother as long as I could remember,"

"What about Mr. Peabody, when did he become your mother's assistant?"

"Shortly after my grandfather passed the business on to my uncle. My mother was furious. She took what was given to her and made her own empire." We picked up our plates and headed to the living room.

"That she did. She's inspiring,"

"I think so too,"

After dinner Samuel and I decided to try and pick up where we left off when I stayed at the mansion. Samuel made the smooth move of scooting next to me and placing his arm around my shoulders. I took it upon myself to help him out and swung my legs across his lap. He looked at me and smiled. I knew he didn't want to do anything wrong or anything I didn't want to do.

"You sure?' He asked while he laid his arm across my waist and pulled me closer.

"I'm good." I responded leaning in for a small peck on his lips.

"Good to know," he said and kissed me deeply as his tongue danced with mine.

As we kissed on the couch, I was excited to have someone who was taking their time with me and wanted to make sure that I was having a good time, not just them. He didn't treat me as if I was supposed to please him, he treated me as if he wanted to please me. Samuel kissed down my neck as I pulled him closer to me. My nipples looked like pebbles in my t-shirt. I had on a pair of thin pajama pants which he quickly slid down the back and squeezed my ass.

"Mmmmmm," I let out a soft moan as he cupped my ass cheek. He made me want to explore more of him as I slid my hand under his shirt and caressed his chest.

He stopped and pulled it over his head, revealing his well built physique, my fingers touching every ripple on his torso. Suddenly his phone began to ring.

"Should you get that?" I asked as it buzzed on the kitchen table.

"Nah, I'm sure it's no one important," he replied and planted a kiss on my lips. "Not as important as you right now."

I blushed. He made me feel so special. I felt so comfortable with him. He ran his fingers through my hair, his fingers gave the soft sensation of pleasure across my scalp. He held the back of my head and pulled me to his lips. He kissed me softly; kissing one lip at a time. Samuel didn't rush getting physical, which is what attracted me to him. He took his time; he knew how to control every moment and every feeling and he knew how to build the passion between us.

His phone frantically rang on the kitchen table, I pulled back and looked at him. I wondered if someone was really trying to get in touch with him.

"Samuel, it sounds like someone is trying to get in touch with you," I said pointing to the phone.

"Yeah, a'ight." He unwillingly removed himself from our embrace to pick up his phone.

"Hello Mother," he said smiling; then his smile suddenly faded. "What do you mean? Are you okay?"

I instantly got chills all over my arms. Something didn't sound right. I slowed my breathing as I wanted to hear everything. I turned towards him and he looked at me. His eyes told me that something had happened and it wasn't good.

"What hospital are you?" he demanded.

Did he say hospital? What the fuck happened?

"I'm on my way." Samuel said and hung up the phone. "Poppie, I have to go. Mr. Peabody has been shot." he said, picking up his coat.

"I'm coming with you." I said slipping on my shoes and grabbing my zip-up hoodie.

Chapter 24 - Payback's a B!tch

BREAKING NEWS: *This is Sandra Rodriguez for Channel 7 ABC News - We interrupt your program to inform you about a shooting that has taken place, possibly involving the Notorious Madame of Chicago, Ms. Vanessa McBride. Our sources inform us that there was a shooting outside of a famous restaurant frequented by many celebrities, politicians and of course the well known Ms. Vanessa McBride of Elegant Industries. And the daughter of the very prominent Mr. Ronald McBride of the outstanding McBride Hotels and Hospitality.*

We have reports that one of Ms. McBride's employees were shot however we cannot confirm that nor are we aware of the condition of the individual that was assaulted. All of this comes on the heels of the on-going investigation regarding Richard Fitzgerald II and one individual employed by Ms. McBride. Everyone is familiar with the ongoing matter of Ms. McBride and her escort service and from what has been the speculation of prostitution within the company.

We will keep you updated as further information is received. You may now return to your regularly scheduled programs.

Vanessa

I can't believe this motherfucker had the audacity to try to fulfill this hit he placed on my head. I got something for him. I couldn't believe Brian took all of those shots for me. He didn't have too, but I knew he would, no matter what. Seeing him on the ground, not moving and me just holding his head - keeps replaying in my head.

Samuel and Poppie came and picked me up from the hospital. I couldn't stay there any longer. I was pissed off and I needed it to be known. Richard needed to know that he has fucked with the wrong Bitch. I was happy Samuel had Poppie to support him right now. Samuel is close to Brian, not like a father, but like a big brother. So I know he might need some support.

As soon as I got to the mansion, I went directly to the office. I waited for Mr. Peabody to follow behind me into my office but he wasn't coming. Just thinking about what happened to him made me furious. Tears swelled up in my eyes as I turned on my computer. Samuel and Poppie entered shortly after.

"Mother, are you okay?"

"I will be. This man must pay for what he has done to me and mine." I said typing furiously on the computer.

"Oh shit," Samuel said. 'Okay, call me if you need anything. Poppie and I will stay here if you need us to."

"I'm good, I have to keep busy to keep my mind off what has happened. If I need you, I'll call, but you two can leave, I'll be fine alone. Set the alarm." I said and went back to typing as they left the office.

I dialed Richard II. He picked up on the second ring - *on speaker phone.*

"Vanessa, how are you? I didn't expect to hear from you. What do I owe this call to?"

"Funny Richard. You knew I was going to call. You already know the answers to your questions,"

"This is true Vanessa. I heard a member of your entourage was shot in a drive-by shooting, it wasn't Mr. Peabody was it?" Richard II scoffed over the phone.

This motherfucker was playing games. I had to let him in a few details and show him that I was the Baddest Bitch in this chess game. I'm the Queen! The most powerful piece on the board and I will not lose at this game.

"Cut the shit Richard. You already know why I'm calling. Where is the settlement?"

"Oh, Vanessa," he laughed and I heard chuckling in the background which I assumed could only be his lawyers which is why he put me on speakerphone. "Yes, I wanted to discuss that,"

"Fuck you Richard. You think I'm playing with you?" I said sternly. "Let me tell you something, you have crossed the wrong Bitch today,"

"Oh Vanessa, don't let our frustrations get the better of you. You might say something that my lawyers will most definitely hear," he said chuckling again over the phone. I was beyond pissed.

I took a deep breath as I knew I wanted to go ballistic on him but I digress. I wanted to make sure what I was about to say resonated with Richard II because I wasn't going to stutter and say it twice.

"Good. I want your lawyers to hear what I have to say. Because from the information that I know, you were involved in the incident." I said, waiting for him to take the bait.

"I'm sorry Vanessa that you think that. You must have gotten your information mixed up. Who told you that I was involved in the shooting?"

"Tavarius Jackson." Richard II instantly picked up the phone. His tone had changed from the man with the biggest balls to a bitch ass motherfucker begging to save his life.

"How do you know about him?"

"Don't worry about it Richard as I need you to listen. I don't appreciate what you've done to one of my employees when you were under contract. This is NOT the first time we've had this discussion. I tried to reason with you and gave you reasonable settlement terms yet you decided it doesn't work for you and you tried to have me killed,"

"I'm sorry...sorry Vanessa. I...I didn't mean...I didn't...."

"Shut the fuck up! I am talking," I demanded. "I'm offended Richard. I thought we had an understanding but apparently, you don't know how this is business and you don't fuck with me and my business. But you took it a step further and tried to have me killed, Richard. Do you understand what that means, Richard?" I asked, waiting for him to respond.

"Vanessa, please....let's talk about this," he begged.

"No more talking Richard. I just want to let you know that I'm coming for you Richard. I'm coming for your Richard the same way you came for me. So watch your back."

"Wait Vanessa," he interrupted.

"And don't think you will be safe in that mansion of yours. I used to fuck your father, I know all of the ins and outs of that fucking building. I know places *you* don't even know. So be prepared Richard, because I'm coming for you!" I said and hung up the phone.

I closed my eyes and tears started to fall. I didn't have Brian with me and I felt absolutely lost. Tonight would be the first night in *years* that I would have to sleep alone. I kept anticipating him coming into my office at any moment but I couldn't hear his footsteps at all like I usually do. His eyes were always so bright when he entered the room. They would fill with love and excitement as soon as he laid his eyes upon mine.

I don't think I am going to get any sleep tonight.

As I sat in my office wishing none of this happened, my phone rang. It was Richard II. I let it ring at least 3 times before I answered.

"Speak."

"Hello Ms. McBride, this is Mr. Ruiz."

"Hello Mr. Ruiz, how can I help you?"

"Yes, We are calling to inform you that the settlement has been paid and an additional 10 million has been added for pain and suffering. We have also agreed to all of the terms stated and

Richard II will no longer be a client of Elegant Industries and is banned from the premises." Mr. Ruiz stated.

"Thank you Mr. Ruiz."

"My pleasure, Ms. McBride." Mr. Ruiz said and he disconnected the phone. I checked the transaction number and he wasn't lying, Richard II had paid $20 Million dollars and settled out of court, as I predicted.

I was happy that he had finally understood the consequences of breaching a contract. What he didn't understand was that this wasn't going to make me go away. He paid what he was supposed to pay, monetarily. Now he must pay for what he has done to me and mine - mentally and physically.

First, I placed $10 million in Poppie's account. She deserved it and so much more. However, I knew she would be satisfied with what she had. Besides, I have something else I want her to do for the company. In the meantime, I downloaded all of the videos we had on Richard II. Every last incident that we have had with him has been recorded and now placed in a compilation video. I've also arranged for the video to be released on every social media platform and news media. I also had the connection with him and Tavarius Jackson released and how he had hired a hitman to kill me to cover up the rape.

I told Richard I wasn't going away quietly and I wasn't going to allow him to think that I was done with him just because he paid the settlement. He planned a hit on me and he violated one of my employees, therefore, he must pay. He needs to understand that when you fuck with the bull, you get the horns. Richard thought that because I was a woman that I would back down against his ass, but he had another thing coming.

The news media channels jumped on it so fast, I'm sure Richard wasn't ready for the shit storm that was coming his way. And with the settlement not mentioning anything about the release of the videos, I was free and clear to do as I pleased. My phone started jumping off as the reporters called in to get confirmation and legitimacy of the video in which I informed them that they were in fact real and the allegations were true.

It wasn't long before Richard II called me complaining that I had taken a low blow by releasing the videos I had of him along with the information about the hit.

"Vanessa! How could you?" Richard II screamed over the phone.

"How could I, Richard?! How could you?!"

"But I paid you!"

"This has nothing to do with the settlement, Richard. This shit is personal. You brought this on yourself." I said and disconnected the phone. I didn't have to explain the shit that he was about to deal with and nor did I want to hear about it. I wanted him to deal with the humiliation that doesn't even compare to what he has done to my ladies, especially Penelope. My phone rang again - it was Poppie.

"Hello Poppie, how are you?"

'Ms. McBride," she said excitedly. "Did you see...um...I just received...uh..Did you know about.." Poppie was so shocked, she didn't know what to say.

"Yes Poppie, it is your compensation for what you had to do through. I'm so sorry sweetheart, I didn't expect that to happen to you and I truly apologize. I know that money can't take away the pain and suffering he caused you, but I hope this can at least compensate for the time you had to be in his presence." I said. I liked Poppie. I knew I would.

"Thank you so much! I've never had this much money before," she said; I could tell she was smiling from ear to ear.

"I understand. No worries, I will have you speak with my financial advisor who will help you manage your money."

"Thank you for everything Ms. McBride. I've never had anyone to care for me like this." I heard Poppie sniff as if she was crying on the other end of the phone.

"It's okay. You have a family now and we take care of our family." I said smiling.

"Thank you again." Poppie said as she disconnected the phone.

Chapter 25 - Support

Samuel was worried about his mother but he knew she was a strong woman. I was worried about him dealing with Mr. Peabody and his mother getting attacked. He came back to my apartment with me, I could only assume he didn't want to be alone.

"Do you think your mother is going to be okay?"

"Yeah, she'll be okay. I'm just worried about the one she's going after,"

"What do you mean?"

"When my mother has that type of look in her eyes, she is going for blood. She knows who did this and she's going after them."

"Oh Shit," I said, my eyes widening.

"Exactly," he said looking at me. "Shit's just getting fucked up,"

"Well you should be strong for your mother, she would want you to." I said and she nodded his head in agreement.

"Thank you Poppie for being there for me, I appreciate it." Samuel said, wrapping his arms around me. It felt so good to be in his warm embrace.

Samuel planted a kiss on my cheek and another on my lips. He lingered a bit, kissing me softly. I wanted to make sure he was okay before we went further, so I let him take the lead. He started to kiss me passionately which led me to believe he was fine. I wrapped my arms around his neck as he found my waist and pulled me closer.

"Can we take this to your bedroom?" Samuel whispered in between kisses.

"Yes," I said softly. I turned, with his hand in mine, I led him to my bedroom. I stood before the end of the bed while he closed the door. Moonlight lit the room softly with a nice blue hue across the walls. Even though it was dark, with our bodies touching each other, we had no issue of seeing.

Samuel held my head gently in one hand as he gave sweet kisses along my neckline. I closed my eyes as his tongue traced the curve of my neck sending chills down my spine.

I slowly unbuckled his belt and opened his pants, he let them fall to the floor and stepped out of them kicking them off to the side. Our lips remained locked as we undressed until we stood before each other; me in my bra and panties and him in his boxer briefs.

I crawled back on the bed and beckoned Samuel to join me. As I laid on my back, he began to kiss my knees as he crawled onto the bed. The closer he got the more my legs opened to invite him to my secret garden.

Samuel kissed my inner thighs softly, my vajayjay quivered the closer he got. I unfastened my bra and freed my girls as he crawled closer to my mound. The intensity between us began to boil hot as he grabbed the sides of my panties and pulled them off.

"Open your legs," he said slowly. It turned me on. It was like him giving me a command and I had no problem fulfilling his request. I slowly opened my legs and waited for his next order.

"Good girl, bend your knees and place them flat on the bed." Samuel ordered and I obliged. My heart started pounding as I waited in anticipation of his next order and move.

"Close your eyes." And I did. I panted as I waited wantonly for his touch to glide across my skin.

I felt him move off of the bed and walk to the side of the bed. He kissed me deeply as his hand held on to one of my girls, him rolling my nipple between his fingers making my love nest shake and my juices began to flow.

"Mmmmmm..." I moaned as his tongue danced with mine.

He quickly replaced his fingers on my pebbled nipple with his mouth, sending a spark between my legs making me wiggle. He licked circles around my nipples, given attention to both as I massaged his member while he leaned against the bed. He was a nice size and I'm sure he knew how to use it well.

He quickly stepped out of his briefs and crawled onto the bed. He kissed my stomach and made a trail as he went towards my southern region. He looked at me as I stroked him, his eyes closing every once in a while enjoying the pleasure I was giving him.

"Mmmm... that feels good," he whispered looking at me. "Please me," he ordered and I took him in my mouth. He inhaled deeply as I sucked him slowly in my mouth, tickling his shaft while he slid further in.

He held himself up and watched me take him in my mouth. I stroked his shaft as I licked around his head which drove him crazy. He bit his bottom lip as I continued to please him. He slid his hand slowly across my mound and with two fingers he spread my fleshy folds to reveal my happy button. He moved his fingers in a circle as he played with my clit forcing me to move my hips.

"Mmmm...you like that," he said as he pulled himself from my mouth. He repositioned himself at the end of the bed and stood watching me while stroking his cock.

"Keep your legs open, don't let your knees fall," he said. I watched as he crawled towards me and kissed my mound. My eyes rolled back in my head as he licked my tulips before parting them with his tongue.

My knees started to fall and then I remembered what he said, instead I moved my feet out farther apart, giving him better access. He buried his face in my love cavern as he sucked my clit, licked my juices while sliding two fingers deep inside my honey pot. My ass lifted it off the bed, my legs wide open as I shook with pleasure as he drank my nectar.

"Ohhhh...ffffuuuuucccckkkk," I moaned as he continued to eat my pussy like it had never been eaten before. My mouth hung open while I pinched my nipples sparking a pulsating pleasure throughout my body.

"Mmmmmmmm...You taste yummy," he said as he kissed my inner thigh steadily sliding is fingers in and out. "Don't come yet baby, hold it." he said as I panted feverishly. He slowly fingered me and wanted me to hold my orgasm.

How much more was I going to take? My damn was about to burst already!

I nodded my head in agreement while he continued.

"Sam....I'm... close baby...I'm....," I moaned. I was almost at the top.

"Hold it baby, hold it," he said as he immediately pulled his fingers from my cave. He climbed quickly between my legs and slid his soldier slowly between my lips and into my sugar canyon. I could feel my walls being stretched by his girth as he continued to fill me completely.

"Uhhhhh.....Mmmmm..." He said as he reached the top. He looked at me and kissed me softly as I wrapped my legs around his waist.

"You feel so good Samuel," I said looking at him. "Make love to me."

"I plan to." Samuel said as he began to move his member in and out of my vajayjay.

Samuel and I rocked back and forth as I felt his cock glide in and out against my velvet walls.

"Oooo...mmmm...mmmmm...mmmm," I moaned as he pumped against me hitting my spot upon every entry.

"Hmmph....Hmmmph...hmppph...mmmm....fuck you feel so good," Samuel said as I used my core muscles to raise my ass off the bed to meet him as he thrusted inward.

"Shit baby...you feel so good inside me..," I knew my flood gates were about to burst as he tapped on the door with the head of his thick cock. He increased his pace and pounded his shaft inside me getting closer to my orgasm.

"Mmmm....baby...don't come...not yet...hold.it..," he panted as he banged forcefully against my mound. "I'm almost there baby,"

"Ahhh....aaahhh...aaah...yes...yes.....baby....come   with me...baby...I can't hold it....aaahhh," I moaned loudly as I had reached my peak.

"Uhhhh....uhhhh....uhhhh....yes...baby...flow all over me baby....let it go baby...," he said and I let it loose.

"Ahhhh...aaaaaaaaaaaaaaahhhhh...yeeessssss baby....uuuhhhh....Fuck!" I cried as I climaxed and opened up the floodgates as my nectar covered his member deep inside me. I could feel my walls squeezing against his shaft as he penetrated me.

"Uhhh...uuhhhh....UUuuuhhhhhhh.....mmmmmmmmmm.....S Samuel said as I could feel his member pulsate and explode deep inside leaving his warm seed oozing within me. He collapsed on top of me, as we rode the pleasure wave to the shore.

His brown skin glistened from the sweat we had created with our love making. It was beautiful. I had never made love before and Samuel was special enough to give that to me. I could feel his heart pounding in his chest as he laid on me trying to catch his breath.

He moved to the side releasing himself from me, I could feel wetness ooze between my legs as gravity helped it to move down the crack of my ass and onto the bed.

"Are you okay?" He asked as laying on his side looking at me. He smoothed my hair back from my face and kissed me softly on the lips.

"I am, thank you. That was wonderful. I've never known how it would feel to make love."

"I'm glad I was able to do that for you," he said, caressing my cheek. "But I'm afraid I didn't use a condom."

"It's okay, I have protection and I'm clean as well."

"I figured you were clean, I didn't know about the protection though." he responded.

"What if I wasn't on anything?" I asked. He seemed as though it didn't phase him.

"Then we would have crossed that line when and if we got to it," he said genuinely.

"Wow, I didn't expect that response,"

"I've never said that to anyone but you." he said looking lovingly into my eyes. He was sincere and honest, I loved that about him.

"I appreciate that, I really do."

"Poppie, I want to be with you, If you'll have me." he said softly hoping I would agree.

"Of course I will have you, you are amazing. I would be crazy not to." I said. He made me feel special and I hadn't had anyone to do that for me. I wasn't going to pass up that opportunity to have a man that would treat me like he does.

"You don't mind me ordering you around?" he asked, his eyes wide hoping I was okay with his domineering side.

"I don't mind it at all. Actually I enjoyed you telling me to hold my orgasm, it made it more exciting." Samuel smiled wide and wrapped his arms around me.

"I want to take you someplace. But let me know if you can't handle anything and we'll stop."

"As long as it's you, I'm fine. I trust you. I know you won't hurt me."

He came in for another kiss and held me close to him. For the first time, I felt wanted, needed and loved. My world had changed so dramatically by one person who saw me as a person who needed a hand.

Later on, on my way back from the bathroom I received a few notifications on my phone and wondered who was trying to reach me. I figured it was Shayla since I hadn't seen her since I got back to my apartment. Yet it was something I least expected. It was a notification from my bank that a deposit had been made. I knew I hadn't expected a deposit in a while unless it was from the settlement that Ms. McBride informed me about it.

I pulled up my banking app and signed in; I looked at the balance and had to sit the fuck down. $10 Million dollars had hit my account! That had to be a mistake. I frantically looked at my text messages to see if Ms. McBride had reached out to me about a mistake that happened, but there was nothing.

$10 Million dollars! That wasn't some chump change, that had to be a mistake. I called Ms. McBride immediately.

"Hello Poppie, how are you?" Ms. McBride answered.

'Ms. McBride," I said excitedly. "Did you see...um...I just received...uh..Did you know about.." I was so shocked, I didn't know what to say.

"Yes Poppie, it is your compensation for what you had to do through. I'm so sorry sweetheart, I didn't expect that to happen to you and I truly apologize. I know that money can't take away the pain and suffering he caused you, but I hope this can at least compensate for the time you had to be in his presence." Ms. McBride said calmly.

"Thank you so much! I've never had this much money before," I said. I was smiling from ear to ear.

"I understand. No worries, I will have you speak with my financial advisor who will help you manage your money."

"Thank you for everything Ms. McBride. I've never had anyone to care for me like this." I started to cry on the other end of the phone.

"It's okay. You have a family now and we take care of our family." she said.

"Thank you again." I said and disconnected the phone.

I sat there for a moment and just realized I was a fucking millionaire!

Thank you God for everything that I went through to get me where I am now.

Vanessa

I couldn't sleep. I was missing him. I needed him. I want to hear him breathing next to me and saying, *'don't go yet, let me hold you a little longer'* when I get up for work. I sat up in the bed and looked over to his side - My Brian was not there.

I got out of bed and slipped on my house shoes. I needed to get out of the house. No one was there and I needed to get out. It felt like there was no life with him not being there with me. Brian has been with me ever since I started my company, my empire. He was there from the very beginning. Brian has supported me and challenged me and grown with me and built a life with me.

As I sat in my car thinking of where to go, I looked at my outfit. It was my half of our matching outfits; a navy blue and orange Chicago Bears jogging suit. I just laughed as I remember going ice skating with Brian at Millenium Park. I drove out the garage as tears began to fall. I drove out the driveway and set my GPS for Northwestern Memorial Hospital.

When I reached the intensive care floor, there was no sound other than the echo of my footsteps on the floor and the beeps of the medical machines. Occasionally I would hear a moan or two coming from the rooms as I walked down the corridor. I heard someone snoring, loud as fuck, with his door wide open. At least one of us was getting some good sleep.

As I neared the room, a nurse exited. She stopped and looked at me with caring eyes.

"Hello Ms. McBride. I figured I would see you here," she said smiling.

"I couldn't sleep." It was all I could say. Tears streamed down my cheeks rapidly the more I spoke or listened to her.

"It's okay. Go right in." The nurse said as she gave me an emotional pat on my shoulders, rubbing up and down on my arm as she walked away.

I slowly entered the room, beeps from the machines greeted me along with a breathing machine. It was breathing for him. My Brian was lying in the bed wrapped in bandages with a tube down his throat to support his breathing. Tears continued to roll down my cheeks as I walked closer to his bed. I held his hand, it was warm but I got no reaction from my touch.

Brian's eyes were closed and he looked lifeless. Other than the machine breathing for him, he wasn't moving. I pulled up a chair next to the bed and held his hand as I leaned against the bed railing.

"Don't leave me Brian," I whispered. "Please don't leave me."

Chapter 26 - Good Day

Weeks passed before Brian was able to be released from the hospital. News reporters were in full force when they caught wind of Mr. Peabody's release. Samuel and Poppie were there with us as we walked out the staff entrance to avoid all of the paparazzi. He held my hand in the SUV as Samuel drove us back to the mansion.

"It's good to have you back Peabody," Samuel said as he parked in the garage.

"It's good to be back," he said, turning and looking at me. Brian kissed the back of my hand and tears swelled in my eyes.

"Yes it is." I responded smiling at him. He was still recovering and still in a bit of pain as he eased out the door while Samuel held it open.

"Are you guys hungry?"

"Yeah, could you order us some food?" I asked Samuel.

"Sure, I'll get enough for everyone." I nodded and slipped my arm around Brian to give him some assistance going into the house.

"Great, you guys are staying. Call us when the food arrives." I said as we entered the house. I was happy Brian had returned and I wanted him all to myself for a moment.

"Where would you like to sit?" I asked as we slowly walked down the hallway.

"I know where I want *you* to sit," he smiled slyly at me. I blushed and giggled.

"You know you can't get physical, you literally just got out the hospital,"

"I know, but my tongue is not hurt at all," he responded, flicking his tongue at me. He chuckled as I knew he was joking, but if only I could. I missed him so much.

"You are so bad,"

"Only for you baby," he said, leaning down and giving me a kiss on my forehead.

"So where are we going in this house because we could walk for miles in here,"

"We can go and chill out in the living room." Brian finally said. We turned towards the living room and sat down on the couch in front of the television.

Brian laid across the chaise and exhaled. He was happy to be home. He looked at me and reached for my hand. I willingly laced my fingers with his and crawled as close as possible to him and focused on his face. I looked at his dark brown eyes and saw the happiness and love he had for me. I ran my fingers along the lines of his face and caressed his cheek. He closed his eyes and held my hand against his face.

"I missed you so much," I said, tearing up. He looked at me and wiped away my tears.

"I know, I missed you too baby,"

"I thought I lost you," I said, crying harder. He instantly wrapped his arms around me and held me tightly as I cried.

"Oh baby, you ain't never gonna lose me," he said, holding me and slightly rocking back and forth. "Ever. I'm not going anywhere."

I believed him. Brian loved me. I've known that for a long time. And I'm sure he knows I love him. I thought I had lost him forever, but he fought to come back to me.

"I'm so glad to have you back," I said smiling through my tears.

"I missed your beautiful face," he said, wiping away my tears. I leaned in and planted a kiss on his lips. I missed his lips. Weeks went by before I was able to just see him look back at me in the hospital. He worked hard to be released, having been on a breathing machine. He was determined.

"I missed yours too."

Samuel and Poppie entered with a huge selection of food he ordered from Calumet Fisheries. He made sure to cover every possible want from fish chips, frog legs, catfish nuggets, stuffed shrimp and a plethora of other items.

"Damn Sam, did you purchase the entire store?" I said looking at the meals they continued to set on the table.

"We wanted to make sure we had a little bit of something for everyone," Poppie said as she sat down on the floor pillows on the other side of the cocktail table.

"I see, well there is something for everyone."

"Everything looks delicious," Brian said as I handed him a container containing an entire meal.

"Good to have you back, Mr. Peabody." Poppie said smiling.

"Please call me Peabody, the same as Sam. It's okay?"

"Aww, thank you. I appreciate that." Poppie smiled and looked at Sam. He leaned over and bumped her playfully.

I noticed the two of them had been closer than ever and I quite enjoyed seeing them together. I knew they would hit it off. I was glad I found her. I thought it was about time to let them in on a little secret that I had been holding on to.

"I have something Samuel I would like to give you and Poppie," Both Poppie and Samuel stopped eating and looked surprised.

"To us?" They said in unison.

"Yes," I pointed at the desk on the opposite side of the room. "Can you look in the first drawer on the right side and bring me the small manilla envelope please?"

Samuel retrieved the envelope and handed it to me as he returned to his seat next to Poppie. I opened the envelope and pulled out a picture of three children - a boy and two girls. I turned it around and showed the picture to both of them. Poppie's eyes instantly widened.

"I have that same picture!" Poppie said pointing towards the picture. I smiled as I had known she would respond first. Sam not so much, he had never seen it before. "That's me and Shayla when we were little. I can't remember the little boy."

"His name is Samuel." I said and both of their eyes widened as they looked at each other. "When you came to live with us, you would always ask if Poppie was coming too," I said looking at the picture.

"Wait, what?!" Sam said, looking at Poppie.

"You would always ask if we could go and pick Poppie up when we would go out to the store, or anywhere you saw other kids, you always wanted to have Poppie by your side," I said looking back at them.

"You searched for me?" Poppie asked, covering her mouth.

"For a very long time. Every chance I got, if I had information on a possibility of where you could be, I searched."

"Wow, I....I don't know what to say," she said.

"I knew if I found you, you would make Samuel happy." I said as she looked at Samuel. He smiled and she caressed his face. "So, I had to find you."

"I didn't know," she said.

"It's okay, we were young, but she found you."

"Yes she did," she said. "Thank you Ms. McBride for finding me. For everything."

"Please, call me Ms. V. The pleasure was all mine. I knew you were a fighter and when I found you, I just had to bring you home with us."

Poppie

Peabody was released from the hospital and was back at the mansion. I was really nice to see him back with Ms. McBride as she looked absolutely lost without him. She brightened up when he was able to leave the hospital as she stayed beside him the entire time.

We were hanging out with them, having lunch after Peabody returned. He allowed me to drop the Mr. from his name, which was a privilege and I was honored. I felt as though I was a part of this family instead of just an employee. I cared for Samuel and he was about to inform his mother about us being together when she threw us for a loop.

Apparently, Ms. McBride had been looking for me for quite some time. She said when she adopted Samuel, he would always ask about a little girl named - *Poppie*. She was given a picture by one of the caretakers at the facility. It was a picture of Shayla, Samuel and me. I had an exact copy and so did Shayla. Shayla and I had forgotten the little boy because he was adopted when we were still kind of young.

"My mother found you," Samuel said, holding my hand.

"She did." I said lacing my fingers with his.

"This time she got it right." Samuel leaned over and kissed my cheek.

As we all hung out in the living room, with Peabody and Ms. V on the couch, Sam and I cuddled together on the numerous floor pillows as they turned on the television.

BREAKING NEWS: *This is Sandra Rodriguez with Channel 7 ABC News - We are interrupting your program to bring you this ongoing situation. Richard Anthony Fitzgerald II has been found dead in a local area motel. Apparently, the disgraced Richard II, son of the Governor Fitzgerald, who has served as Governor of Illinois for years, was found dead by an individual named Sparkle. As information is steadily coming in, our sources stated that the individual, Sparkle, was a well known prostitute, yet that is yet to be confirmed.*

Again, Richard Anthony Fitzgerald II has been found deceased in a local area motel. As we know he has been in the news for almost the past two months as charges have been filed against rape, assault and battery, extortion and conspiracy for a murder for hire plot against the Notorious Vanessa McBride. Informational evidence flooded the media reports shortly after the murder for hire took place ending in Ms. McBride's assistant getting attacked and hospitalized.

Ironically, her assistant was released today and is home resting from this ordeal.

A full autopsy report will be done to determine the cause of death, which should be released in a few weeks.

We will bring you more information as it comes into the studio. This is Sandra Rodriguez with Channel 7 ABC News. You may now return to your regularly scheduled program.

We turned around and looked at Peabody and Ms. V; they were frozen looking at the t.v. He was dead. Richard II was dead. That was so unexpected.

"Good riddance to bad rubbish." Ms. V said as she looked at the t.v. She was happy he was dead and so was I.

Today was a good day. He was gone, finally. He wouldn't bring any more problems to Ms. V. Peabody was back and recovering and I got paid for dealing with that motherfucker. It's amazing how shit fell apart for him as quickly as it did. Apparently, with him being banned from the company and its properties he lost all credibility when the video was released and his world took a downward spiral.

The Governor had disowned him shortly after the video was released from what I thought, but Ms. V told us that he had been disowned from the incident with me. His own father distanced himself from him to avoid any implications that might arise.

"Absolutely. Is it too early to have a toast?" I asked. Ms V smiled at me.

"A woman after my own heart," she said as she got off the couch heading for the mini bar on the opposite side of the room. She brought back a tray holding 4 shot glasses and a bottle of Don Julio 1942 Anejo.

We all took a shot of tequila and dedicated it to good health, good business and good love.

Epilogue

Poppie

After the announcement of Richard II being found dead in the hotel, it wasn't long after the autopsy report was revealed. It was found that Richard II had a plethora of drugs in his system, one of them, Fentanyl, which contributed to his death. I wasn't surprised to be honest, I figured he was on something when I first met him at his mansion.

Ms V was cleared of any wrongdoing and business was back to normal. However, Shayla and I were promoted to Recruiting in which we were now the individuals who invited the ladies to join our company. I gave Shayla $3 million dollars of my money that I got from the settlement. She didn't want it but I told her if it wasn't for her, I wouldn't be here and I wasn't going to take 'no' for an answer.

Ms. V and Peabody are happy as ever together as they should be. I heard through the grapevine that she let go of all of her clients and passed them onto others within the company and Peabody no longer hooks up with the ladies. It's good to see them commit themselves to each other; honestly it was about time.

Samuel and I moved in together and we have grown so much in our relationship. We love each other so much. This was something I've wanted for a long time. The sex is immaculate as he introduced me to a world that I love, but only with him. I love that we have something special we share together which makes our relationship stronger.

Finally, I've found my place in the world. I've found my home.